What I Know Now

What
I
Know
Now

RODGER LARSON

Henry Holt and Company

New York

Henry Holt and Company, Inc.
Publishers since 1866
115 West 18th Street
New York, New York 10011

Henry Holt is a registered
trademark of Henry Holt and Company, Inc.

Copyright © 1997 by Rodger Larson
All rights reserved.
Published in Canada by Fitzhenry & Whiteside Ltd.,
195 Allstate Parkway, Markham, Ontario L3R 4T8.

Library of Congress Cataloging-in-Publication Data
Larson, Rodger.
What I know now / Rodger Larson.
p.   cm.
Summary: In 1957 in California, having fallen in love with a young man who has come
to his house to build a garden, a fourteen-year-old boy with homosexual yearnings
finds his life and his worldview changing.
[1. Homosexuality—Fiction. 2. Gardens—Fiction. 3. California—Fiction.] I. Title.
PZ7.L32395Wh   1997   [Fic]—dc20   96-36723

ISBN 0-8050-4869-3
First Edition—1997

Printed in the United States of America
on acid-free paper. ∞

10 9 8 7 6 5 4 3 2 1

For Andy and for Liz

Acknowledgments

It's said that writing is a lonely and solitary craft. True enough, I figure. It's also said that when writers write they are surrounded by everyone they have known, been taught by, influenced by—the whole human parade. I figure that's true, too. As a writer, I'm indebted to all those folks who surround me while I work alone.

My debt is great; so is my gratitude.

Thank-you to my mother, Inez, and my father, Ernest, for the wonders of the childhood they provided and for their influence. Thank-you to my brother, Paul, who shared that childhood and no doubt remembers it differently. Thank-you to his sons, Steve and Jeff. Thank-you to my aunt, Helen Wright. Thanks to another aunt and uncle, Elsie and Leslie Ogden. Thanks to Sharon Wiseman and Curt Wright, cousins as close as sister and brother to me.

Thanks to Tom Spanbauer, who brought me to my voice and taught me to "word it."

Thanks to every dang one of the Dangerous Writers. What a crew. And especially, thanks to the Quintet: Helen Beum, Ann Buckingham, Kathleen Concannon, and Rachel Hoffman.

Thanks to my friends, those folks who are more family than family: Sarah Cook and Shirlee Geiger, Susan Dobrof and Paul McKee, Jin Darney and Craig Johnson, Sue Lynn and Sorca O'Connor, Michael O'Rourke and Mary Orr, MC

Lamb, Daryl Johnson, and Sandy Polishuk, who is my poetry reading buddy as well.

Thanks to the folks from my Antioch program: Barbara Drake, Sandra Williams, and Jon Saari.

Thanks to my agent, Charlotte Sheedy, and to my editor, Marc Aronson. Thank you, thank you.

From my experience at Evergreen, thanks to Howard Waskow, Frank Motley, and Bill Bruner—more than educators, mentors, too.

From other times and places, Marjorie Cutting, Bonnie Partch, Jim Heynen, Andrea Carlisle, and Martha Gies.

Thanks to two men who taught me about myself, Michael Hennon, Robert Nichols.

Thank-you to the writing folks in workshops I've attended and given. The work is difficult, at times it seems too much, but it isn't. It's worth it. Thanks to the students at Metropolitan Learning Center; I'm a student there, too.

Thanks to Gayl Larson, and especially to Elizabeth Larson.

And from way, way down in my heart, thanks to Andy Simon for all that he does and is. My buddy. Thanks.

What I Know Now

Prologue
Stockton,
Summer 1957

 IT WAS THE SUMMER AFTER THE
spring my mother and father decided to live separately. The
summer I moved with my mother to the Home Place
where my mother's mother had lived until she died. This
was the same summer my brother stayed with my father out
on the ranch, because my brother was the older son, and
my father said he needed him to help with haying and the
harvest. It was the summer of 1957 when I turned fourteen
and I met a man named Gene Tole, who worked at the Central Valley Nursery. Gene Tole came to the Home Place to
build a garden for my mother and I fell in love with him, but
didn't know it at the time.

I suppose that was the most important thing about that
summer, falling in love with Gene Tole, because after that in

some way I didn't feel like the same person anymore. But maybe that feeling of being different was because of my parents being separated, and my not seeing my brother, or because of my moving closer to town and starting a new school in the fall. Who knows? But by the end of the summer I wasn't the same anymore.

Who
We
Are
Becoming

 WHEN IT CAME TIME TO LEAVE THE ranch, I thought of the things I would miss. I sat in my mother's old green Packard in the dark shed next to the tank house where my mother kept her car. Early in the morning, I opened the doors to the shed and put big, smooth river rocks in front of both doors to keep the wind from blowing them shut. I carried packed boxes out of the house and put them in the trunk. When the trunk was full I put the rest of the boxes on the backseat. Then I got in the Packard and sat there on the shotgun side waiting in the dark for Ma, and I thought of the things I would miss.

I would miss the walnut trees to climb, the smooth, white, skinlike bark, the ease their limbs offered for leaving the ground, and the cool shade. And there was Little John

Creek, which wandered through the ranch near the southern fence line. I'd miss the raft my brother, Brad, and I had on Little John Creek that we poled across the muddy water or along its slimy banks, playing Huck and Jim when we were younger; and trying to catch turtles that were, for such slow creatures, the fastest things I'd ever seen once they read your mind and understood that you wanted to catch them and take them home to be your pet.

Before long I got restless and left the car and the garage and walked across the bare gravel yard into the orchard and under the walnut trees, leaves still small and bright green, tiny walnuts hanging from twigs. The dirt was disked smooth and easy to walk on. No big clods to kick. Irrigation dikes and ditches weren't in place yet; it was still too close to spring for the need to irrigate.

The orchard ended in a curved line which was the bank of Little John Creek, and I stood there on the bank and looked south across the muddy water at the vast open field.

The land here is flat. The horizon of the valley floor is so distant that on most days the natural boundaries of the landscape disappear. The foothills of the Sierra Nevada rise up in the east, too far away to be seen, and to the west on a clear day Mt. Diablo is just a flat silhouette, jutting up, looking for all the world like someone propped it there—the backdrop of a stage set placed at the edge of San Francisco Bay. The least bit of haze blocks it out.

This is where I lived all my life, fourteen years, until now.

Along the slough where I walked there was no sign of the raft Brad and I played on as kids. Long gone, I guess. The turtles were missing, too, still buried in mud to avoid the winter cold. Across the slough in the distance there was an oak tree.

I would miss the huge valley oak trees; they were the tallest thing in the empty fields of the ranch. And I would miss being under those trees, where the grass was thick and rich in the summer because cattle liked the shade of the oak trees, too, and cow pies fertilized the soil, making whatever grew there lush and thick.

I would miss the windmills. They stood up on the land, catching energy from the air and using it to pump wonderful clear water from the ground into the watering troughs for the cattle to drink and for me to run my hands through and splash on my face on hot days.

And the cracks in the soil, I'd miss those places—sinkholes, my father called them—where the clay would crack and curl and you could peel a top layer off the earth like a scale, a checked piece of reptile skin. I'd miss these things and other things I wasn't thinking of just yet.

I tried not to think about my father and my brother. Didn't want to think about them, missing them. I was sitting on the bank of Little John Creek, throwing dirt clods into the water, hoping to scare up a turtle or two, knowing you don't scare a turtle up: if you scare a turtle, you scare it down. That's when Ma started calling me; at least it's when I first heard her.

"Dave, Dave." Her voice was faint and stretching out in the air, stretching between the limbs of walnut trees.

"Dave, where are you?"

"I'm coming," I hollered. I ran through the orchard toward the house, no thought of the things I'd miss—trees, raft, windmills—in my head now, the only thought of Dad and my brother, Brad. Leaving them.

"What were you doing out there?"

"Looking at the slough, thinking," I said.

"Why don't you get in the car," Ma said. "I'm going to check the house one more time."

When she was ready to leave, Ma came into the shed where I was sitting in the car, put her suitcase on the boxes in the backseat, and sat behind the wheel of her old Packard—the car that had been her mother's car.

"That's it," she said.

My mother put her arm over the back of the seat and turned around, looking out the rear window as she backed the car out.

"Shall I close the doors?" I asked.

"Leave them open," she said. "Leave the damn things wide open."

We headed out of the yard, down the gravel road, plumes of dust rising behind the wheels of the Packard and drifting slowly toward the walnut grove. The dust is bad for the walnuts, my father said, because it causes red spiders to come and they eat the leaves. Ma didn't care.

We turned onto Jack Tone Road. It was a route we had

taken hundreds of times before—the road to Stockton—but this time was different: we weren't coming back. We both knew it.

Ma was driving along on Jack Tone Road now, and tears streaked down her cheeks and she said "Shit" every once in a while. I didn't say anything. I didn't want to think yet about why we were leaving the ranch, about what leaving would mean to us.

"I don't know how important it is that we're leaving things behind," my mother said. We were both silent for a while.

Ma and I drove across the Mormon Slough on the white-washed bridge. We went past Star Hatler's place, Minihan's, and Thompson's.

"We'd best look ahead," she said. "To who we are becoming." It was quiet in the car, and the words *who we are becoming* filled the air, empty and yet heavy in the soft rumble of tires on pavement.

I rolled down the window to feel the cool morning breeze in my face and let the breeze blow through my fingers and around my hand and on my hair.

By the time we passed the Berger place, and before the Sanganetti place, my mother pulled the Packard over to the side of the road and took a handkerchief out of her purse, which sat on the seat between us, blew her nose hard a couple of times, wiped her eyes and cheeks, and said, "Well, that's a finished chapter."

She put the hanky back in the purse and took a tube of

lipstick out. She stretched over toward my side of the car, looked in the rearview mirror and painted her lips. Then she moved her lips together to seal the paint job. She dropped the lipstick tube back in the purse, said "Screw 'em," and gunned the Packard. We spun a cloud of dirt into the air, gravel pinged on the fender wells. We were back on the road, on our way to the Home Place, on our way to who we were becoming.

Ma was quiet for a long time as she drove the Packard along Farmington Road toward Stockton.

After a while she said, "We can paint the house at the Home Place. Build a garden."

We went past Old Mrs. Bryant's, where peacocks lived in the trees around her house, past the Hollenback place, Osage orange trees a windbreak along the fence line.

We crossed the Southern Pacific railroad tracks, drove past Kato's truck farm, past Moore Equipment Company, the El Rancho Motel, Montezuma School. We turned right onto Mariposa Road and drove the last three miles in silence.

My mother slowed the car, held her arm straight out the window to signal left, and we turned onto the gravel driveway at the Home Place, 1707 on the mailbox, drove past the black walnut tree, dust rising from the gravel. Ma pulled up to the barn beside the house and stopped the car. We sat for a moment. Looked across the seat at each other.

"Well, here we are," Ma said. She got out of the Packard

and took her suitcase from the backseat. She walked across the driveway and set the suitcase on the bottom stair to the side porch. Ma stepped back a few paces and looked up at the old homestead. She walked slowly toward the front of the house, looking at the porch, at the second story, at the little wrought-iron fence that went around the top part of the roof.

Ma's footsteps sounded on the front stairs. She came back from the front porch, walking along the side porch to where I was standing in the driveway. I put my thumbs under my belt and hiked up my Levi's.

"The old house needs paint," Ma said. "And a big rambling garden around it. All these porches. Imagine. Climbing roses, jasmine," she said. "Can't you just see it? An English country garden."

"Yeah," I said. But I couldn't. I couldn't see it at all. Paint was peeling off the shingle siding. Shingles were falling off as well. Dry weeds were all around the house, right up to the brick foundation.

"Shall I carry the boxes in?" I hiked up my Levi's again.

"May as well," Ma said. She came down the stairs and picked up her suitcase and carried it into the house.

Barefoot

 MA WALKED THROUGH THE OLD house, stopping at windows to pull back curtains, roll up shades. Her figure showed tall and graceful moving through the large rooms. Stuck windows didn't stand a chance; they were no match for Ma's strong shoulders and long arms. She pushed windows open, weights thumping gently in the hollow sashes. She propped the doors outside open. The house got sized up like she was a sergeant major.

"I never thought I'd be back here like this," Ma said, mostly to herself. She ran her hand through her curly brown hair.

Every once in a while she picked something up and said, "For Pete's sake."

Dust covered everything and light from the windows showed how shabby the rooms and furniture were.

"I'm going to take the downstairs bedroom," Ma said. "You pick one upstairs. Not the room over mine; I don't want to hear you wandering around up there when I'm trying to sleep."

"I'll take Uncle Richard's room," I said.

Uncle Richard's room was in the back of the house and had three dormers, each facing a different direction. One dormer had an overstuffed armchair and a metal reading lamp in it. I walked into the dormer with the writing desk and looked out the window. The ceiling sloped down to the wall, which was only four feet high—all the surfaces, except the floor and windows, were tongue and groove siding, which felt good on my fingers as I slid them along the wall, each groove only a couple of inches from the next. The wood was stained rosy brown.

"Bring the sheets from up there," Ma hollered. "I'll get a load of wash going so we have fresh things for tonight. Then I'm starting on the kitchen."

I opened the windows, then plopped down on the double bed; scrolls of dust puffed out like you'd see in a cartoon. Cobwebs hung from the ceiling, clustered in the corners. I got up and looked in the bureau drawers. They were empty, lined with faded newspapers—blotched brown in places and stiff.

It was Grandma who called this Richard's room. Uncle

Richard had lived here when he was a boy, he lived here until he went away to the war and got killed. Pictures of Uncle Richard were in the family albums, but otherwise he was gone, dead in Italy before I was born. No one talked about him anymore.

Stale newspaper, smell of dust, thoughts of Uncle Richard . . . My chest felt like bits of hard stuff were falling inside and piling up, clogging my throat. I wandered back to the bed and lay down, looked out the window into a locust tree, fresh yellow-green leaves.

"Shit," I said.

I hit my fist hard on the bed and dust flew into the air, lying there in the upstairs bedroom saying "Shit" over and over, dust clouds filling the air. I coughed and then laughed until I couldn't say "Shit" anymore, and tears were running down my cheeks from coughing and laughing so much and I started to cry. Said "Shit" a few more times and after a while felt better. Stayed upstairs and thought about what to do with this room to make it mine.

The bedclothes came off with just a couple of yanks and I separated the sheets and bedspread from the blankets. I tucked the sheets and spread under my arms and took them down the back stairs to the kitchen.

"Put them in the washer on the back porch," Ma said. She had a bucket in the sink, was getting ready to mop the kitchen floor. She already had her bedclothes in the washer and it was filling with water, soap in there, too; where she got the soap, I didn't know.

I stayed with the washing machine for a while. The tub filled with water and I shut the faucet off over the wash trays. Moved the lever over to start the agitator swishing back and forth, put my hand in there a bit to push the bed-clothes down, a real no-no in Ma's list of things not to do from when I was a kid, but I felt like living dangerously. Then I put the lid on the tub and set the timer to go off in fifteen minutes, plenty of time to get the sheets and pillow-cases agitated clean.

In the kitchen, over by the far wall, Ma was standing with her shoes and socks off, standing in her bare feet, mopping the linoleum floor. Bare feet shouldn't be a big deal, but in my family they were. Dad had a rule: "Go barefooted, sure as hell you'll get flat feet," he said. "Sure as hell you'll step on a rusty nail. Get lockjaw."

Dad's rule was for Brad and me; it included no sneakers, no sandals, slippers only at bedtime. Ma never went without shoes except maybe when she got out of the shower and had her bathrobe on—still, I had no idea the rule applied to her.

"You don't want to get your shoes wet, Ma?"

"I don't," she said, "but mostly it feels good."

She looked at her feet, wiggled her toes up and down as if they were playing scales on a piano. She took the mop out of the bucket, soapy water sloshed on the floor.

"It just feels good," she said.

She dipped one foot in the mop bucket, then the other. She stood in the soapy water on the linoleum and moved her feet back and forth as if she were doing the jitterbug. Her feet squeaked on the wet floor and her hand moved the mop handle like a dance partner and she flipped her faded housedress back and forth at her side while she danced around.

"Want to help?"

"Sure," I said.

"All right, but don't get your shoes wet. Better roll up your Levi's, too."

Early in the afternoon Ma said she was going out to get some supplies.

"Find the ladder in the tank house—I'm sure it's there—and take down the curtains in the living room and dining room. I'll wash them when I get back."

"Okay," I said.

"Be careful of black widows out there in the tank house, you know. The tank house has always been thick with them. Bats, too. Bats have rabies. Be careful."

"Great. Anything else I should know?"

"I think that about covers it." She laughed. "I'll be back in half an hour."

I stood in the middle of the kitchen until the sound of Ma's car, tires on gravel, died away. Then I eased slowly through the back porch, resting my hand on the washing machine, tracing the edge of the concrete wash tray with my finger, and opened the screen door. Standing at the top of the back steps, I stared across the open ground at the door to the tank house fifteen feet away. I went down the stairs and walked along the brick walkway, which led to the wooden door.

The air where I walked felt thicker than air, holding me back, as if I were walking in a slow-motion dream.

At first the tank house door wouldn't open. I pulled and pounded and finally lifted up and yanked at the same time and it came loose. On the inside, two stairs went down to the dirt floor.

The stairs ended at a small cleared place, a path through generations of junk. I stood on the dirt floor, not moving, waiting for my eyes to adjust to the dark. Even then I couldn't see the bats, which I knew were hanging from the rafters two and a half stories above me. I didn't mind bats, they had to live somewhere. One time I had a chance to touch a bat; it was in an enamel dishpan on the workbench in the tank house. The bat was tiny; a baby bat, perhaps, that went into the dishpan to catch an insect and got trapped there by the slick enamel sides. The bat was so weak it couldn't fly when I took it outside, dishpan and all, to toss it to freedom like it was dirty dishwater.

Above me specks of light shone sharp through tiny cracks where the shingles that covered the outside of the tank house didn't quite meet. I was looking up from the bottom of what felt like a pitch-black hole, that's what I was doing, and wishing I was somewhere else, wishing I wouldn't upset the black-widow spiders that lived there, while they bit the heads off their husbands and got ready to eat the rest of their husbands' bodies before they set about spinning nests to lay eggs and hatch a bunch more black-widow spiders that would make the tank house I didn't want to enter their home.

When my eyes adjusted I saw the workbench along one wall, with only a couple of feet of bare space where you could see the workbench itself, the rest piled with junk. Behind the workbench were shelves of glass jars with nuts, bolts, rivets, and screws in them. Tin boxes with pipe fittings, washers, and cotter pins were on the shelves, too. A wooden box with dovetailed corners was full of porcelain doorknobs, hinges, and latches. A gallon can for turpentine stood empty on the shelf; the turpentine evaporated years ago, before my grandmother died. These were the parts, the project leftovers, the "you can't throw that away, you never can tell when we're going to need something just like that" things of my grandmother's life.

Farther back in the tank house, rusty garden tools hung on the wall or were propped against the wall or lay on the floor where they had fallen. Among the tools was an eight-foot wooden ladder. I kicked the tools on the floor a little to warn the black-widow spiders; I didn't want to surprise a black widow with my hand. I moved the tools aside to get to the ladder. Finally, I got to the ladder and pulled it away from the tools.

I backed out of the tank house, trying not to upset anything, especially not the spiders. I left the bats, the black-widow spiders, and the generations of junk, came outside, to be blinded by the sunlight while I stood on the brick walkway between the house and the tank house, to let my eyes adjust to reenter the world.

Female
Technique

THAT EVENING MA AND I HAD
breakfast for supper—scrambled eggs, bacon, and fresh
sliced tomatoes. We had chunky applesauce with lots of cinnamon on top for dessert and store-bought peanut-butter
cookies. When the dishes were done, we sat in the living
room for a while and Ma turned the radio on.

After a bit she said, "It's been a big day, I'm going to take
a bath and go to bed." Ma looked tired. Her voice was soft
and sad-sounding. She put her hands in her hair and pulled
pins out that held her hair in a loose knot. Her hair was dark
and wavy, and fell around her shoulders and down her back.

"I'm going to bed, too," I said. "See you in the morning."

I climbed the stairs to my room and sat in the stuffed
chair in the dormer, took off my shoes and considered the

day, which seemed like about three days. I was thinking about how hard the day must have been for Ma and how tired she looked and sad she sounded, and I decided to go downstairs and tell her I was glad we were here and that we could fix the old house up spiffy and make it good for ourselves here.

When I got downstairs in my bare feet, the house felt eerie, all quiet and dark, the only light a bit that seeped from around the bathroom door in the front hall. I picked my way carefully, feeling the walls and the chairs, not wanting to knock anything over, planning the words to say through the wall to Ma. Then from the bathroom came the high, breaking sound of Ma crying.

I waited in the living room, stood still, unsure of what to do. Listened to the cries and sobs and to the silence. My legs felt weak. Without saying anything, without calling out or trying to calm her, I climbed upstairs, leaving her alone in the bath.

The bedroom window was open and a breeze caught in the lace curtain and billowed it out over my bed, where I lay with no clothes on. I gave up on sleep and played with the curtain in my hand, letting the curtain drift about. And I thought of Brad. I thought of a time with Brad in the walnut orchard on the ranch when we played together. Brad was probably ten and I was seven.

The place where we played was called the settling tank and was forbidden to us. I wasn't sure why. It seemed safe enough to me. But it was one of the places on the ranch where we were told never to go.

The day Brad and I went there was a hot day. It was a day of endless sun and still, breathless air. The leaves on the walnut tree hung limp, unmoving, their color dull and dusty.

We were lying on the sandy bottom of an irrigation ditch, which was still slightly moist and cool from the last irrigation, looking up through the walnut tree leaves, and Brad said, "I know what they're called."

"What what's called?" I said.

"You know."

"I don't," I said. "I don't know."

It was important to say everything right. I could tell Brad needed to talk about something important, and I wanted him to tell me what it was.

"You know," he said. "A woman's private place."

"What's it called?" I said.

We were quiet.

"What's it called? A woman's private place?" I said.

The stillness and quiet of the trees and the death of the air settled around us. It held me down, pressing me into the soft, sandy soil of the irrigation ditch.

"Pussy," Brad said. "The place between their legs, it's called a pussy."

"What?" I said. "That doesn't make any sense. Why would anybody call a place between their legs a pussy?"

"I don't know. I guess because it's soft. Maybe because it's furry."

"Furry?" I said.

Brad didn't say anything more. My breath was short and quick.

"How'd you find out?" I asked.

"At school. Tony Bonfelio. One of Bonfelio's hired men told him. Tony saw a magazine, too."

"What kind of magazine?" I said.

"A nudist camp magazine. Tony said all the good parts were blanked out."

I kept quiet and hoped Brad would say more. He was funny about what he'd say and not say; too much of anything, quiet or question, could cause him to clam up like you wouldn't believe.

"I guess some people call that place a bulldog," he said. "But I can't figure that out. Why they'd call it a bulldog. You got any idea?"

"No," I said.

Then, although neither my brother nor I said, "Let's go to the settling tank," we got up and walked toward the back of the shed where the walnut huller was kept. The tank was behind the shed. Brad and I climbed the homemade ladder up the side of the concrete tank, threw our legs over the thick wall, and let ourselves down into the cool quiet inside. We climbed down the ladder until it stopped and then dropped the last few feet to the soft silt built up on the bottom.

This is how the tank worked. It was a rectangle, twelve feet by eight feet, and fourteen feet high. The tank was divided in two by a concrete baffle. The pump used to irrigate the walnut orchard pumped directly into one side of the tank. This water carried silt with it, which settled to the bottom. When the water rose to the square hole in the concrete baffle, it began filling the other side of the tank, where more silt settled to the bottom. Here the outlets to the irrigation lines were arranged like portholes high along the wall, where silt would not get out into the irrigation lines and clog them. Metal wheels on top of the tank were turned to control the water released into the orchard. Metal plates were bolted over holes in the tank sides near the bottom, where silt was shoveled out when it built up too high.

It was the most pleasant place on the ranch to be on a hot day. We could play in the sand and wade in the cool, fresh water collected there.

Brad took off his shoes and socks and rolled up his Levi's. I did the same. We played in the sand, molding it with our hands, scooping it around into roads and ditches like we usually did. Then my brother took off his T-shirt and his Levi's and hung them on the bottom rung of the ladder. I did the same. We didn't talk much.

"You play here," he said.

Brad climbed through the square hole in the concrete baffle that separated the two parts of the settling tank. I looked through the square hole after him. There was more water on his side than on mine, but I didn't care. I built some more roads and made a channel where ships could go into a port from the water puddle in the corner of the tank. I got up to check on what Brad was doing on his side and I was surprised to see that he had hung his underwear on the square hole between us. I took off my underwear, too, and jumped up and crawled through to his side. The rough edge of the concrete scraped my stomach and thighs. I didn't care.

Brad sat near the water on moist sand.

"Want to see my female technique?" he said.

"Sure." I sat down beside him.

He spread his legs out flat in a V before him. With his hands he pulled moist silt up between his legs. The silt covered his penis. His penis disappeared.

I liked what he had done, and I did exactly the same. It felt good, the cool, moist silt on my penis.

Then my brother lay back in the silt and he took a large handful of sand and put it over his nipple and cupped it and patted it until it was smooth and only cracked a little, and then he took a small pinch of sand and put it right on top.

"A tittie," he said.

I began to make one for myself, over my nipple.

Brad was making a second.

"Another tittie," he said when he was done.

Brad and I lay like that in the bottom of the irrigation tank, feeling the cool comfort of the damp silt, wiggling our toes once in a while. I thought about our female technique.

Then Brad sat up and brushed what remained of his sand titties off his chest. He moved up on his knees and shook the sand off his penis. Then he went into the pool of water in the corner of the tank and washed himself off. I did the same. I was hoping for more information. I wondered how I could see the nudist magazine Tony Bonfelio had seen.

"Let's dry off on the roof," Brad said.

He climbed through the square window in the baffle. I followed. My brother helped me reach the first rung of the ladder and then he handed me my clothes and I began to climb out of the settling tank, my clothes held over my shoulder.

I stepped off the ladder on the outside of the irrigation tank onto the roof of the shed where the walnut huller was kept. The roof, like the other shed roofs, had a steep section and a more level section. The orchard came right up to the shed and a large limb of one of the walnut trees hung over the shed roof and made it impossible to see from the yard during the summer when the tree leafed out. I sat down on the roof where the steep part and the gentle part met, leaning my back against the steep part. The roof was made of cedar shingles, and moss grew in the grooves between the shingles. When it was cooler and damper, the moss was a bright green, but now it was dull and dark brown.

Brad came and sat down beside me. The hot air around us felt good after the the cool of the settling tank and the splash bath we had from the pool there.

"I wonder why people would call it a bull dog," Brad said.

"Beats me."

"Wish we could see that magazine Tony saw," he said.

I thought about the picture Dad had on the wall of the

bunkhouse of a lady sitting on her knees on a puffy white fur rug holding an apple, leaning forward so her breasts hung way out and were all pink and rosy, and her cheeks looked pink and rosy, too, and all over she looked pink and rosy like she had just been scrubbed. She looked too perfect to be real. And she wasn't showing anything real. You could see more "real" than that in a *National Geographic*.

"Want to see my female technique again?" Brad said.

He jumped up and brushed off his butt where he had been sitting on the cedar shingle roof. Then, facing me, my brother opened his legs and reached around behind his back and with his hand pulled his penis back between his legs and held it there until he moved his legs close together. With his penis held this way, he began to strut along the roof right under the limbs of the walnut tree. He turned around and strutted back in front of me.

"What do you think?"

"Does it really look like that?" I asked.

My brother let his penis slip out from between his legs. His penis was slightly swollen and larger than usual. He didn't answer.

"Want to see my female technique?" I asked.

Brad didn't say anything, so I stood up and reached around and pulled my penis back under my body and between my legs and then closed my legs together to hold it there. I tried strutting my technique along the shed roof, too. I knew that even though the moss on the roof was dry and not as slick as it was at other times of the year, it was still slippery and I could fall and slide off the roof. I stopped under one of the walnut tree limbs and put my hand over it, limp wristed, to hold on and at the same time look alluring. I held my other arm in front of my nipples in provocative modesty. I swung my hip to one side.

"What do you think?"

"I don't know."

Brad was looking down. He didn't seem interested in me or my female technique. He looked embarrassed.

My brother pulled his penis between his legs again and came toward me. I took my hand from being draped over the walnut tree limb and waddled toward my brother. We moved around in a circle, like we were dancing, but we didn't touch. I put my arm out in a vampish move. We continued in our circle. I put my hand over Brad's shoulder and then I put my arm around his neck. I put my face next to Brad's face, my penis still held between my legs, and I rubbed my cheek against his cheek, like I had seen grown-ups do when they were dancing.

"You're a creep," my brother said.

He pushed me back and I slipped on the cedar shingle roof and slid a short way toward the edge on the dried moss. When I turned around Brad was bending over picking up his undershorts and stepping into them. I could see that now his penis was large and pinker than I'd ever seen it before.

"What's the matter? It's only female technique," I said.

"You're a creep, a sissy," Brad said. He was pulling his Levi's on.

2 8

I didn't know what I could say.

"I was only playing," I said. I wished my brother would turn around and we could play some more.

"It's only a game."

"Well, I don't want to play," Brad said.

"It's your game."

"Well, I'm not playing it anymore. I'm not playing it ever again," he said.

My brother pulled his T-shirt over his head and down over his chest. He climbed down the ladder and ran away somewhere where I couldn't find him, and I didn't see him again that day until my mother called us to come in to supper.

I thought about it now, lying in bed at the Home Place trying to fall asleep. Thought about my brother, Brad, and the irrigation tank, thought about pussy, thought about female technique. I lay in bed moving my hand against the lace curtain and the evening breeze like they were lazy water in a slow stream. I pulled the top sheet back and forth across my body, rubbing it against my penis, my penis hard now, standing above my stomach, and I moved my hand over it, feeling so good until it was over and then I felt the shame again that I felt when my brother called me a creep and a sissy and left me on the shingle roof of the shed where the walnut huller was kept.

Gene

 THE DAY I MET GENE TOLE MY mother said, "I'm on my way to visit Vivian Bowers. You want to come along?"

"No," I said. "I'll just stay here."

I was reading *Lydia Bailey* by Kenneth Roberts. The cover of *Lydia Bailey* had a sexy picture of a lady in a low-cut dress, all pulled apart and torn, but I hadn't come to any sexy scenes yet. I was still reading it, though, in hopes of finding some.

"I want you to come along," Ma said. "It'll do you good to get out of the house."

"I don't want to, Ma."

"Go put your shoes on."

I went upstairs to put my shoes on, looked in the mirror and combed my hair a bit.

Ma had the Packard backed out of the shed and waiting in the driveway when I came outside. I got in the shotgun seat and pulled the door closed with a solid thud.

I rolled down my window as Ma drove out the driveway and the fresh air blew the smell of the leather seats away, blew the smell of rose water and powder away, too, my mother's smell.

"I'm glad you've come along. I want you to see what a real garden is like. I can't wait to see Vivian's garden myself."

Ma had met Vivian Bowers at the garden club. Vivian owned the Central Valley Nursery.

"Everyone I've talked to at the garden club says Vivian is a world-class gardener," Ma said.

What exactly "world class" meant to the women of the Stockton Garden Club I didn't know. Didn't ask, either.

"A young man named Gene Tole works for Vivian in her garden and at the nursery," Ma said. "According to Vivian, Gene has a degree in horticulture. I talked to him on the telephone about building a garden for us at the Home Place. He'll probably be working in Vivian's garden this afternoon. We'll have a chance to meet him."

"Oh," I said.

We drove through an ordinary neighborhood, small bungalow-style houses and larger ones, mostly old, some run-down, and every once in a while a vacant lot with weeds and trees. Ma slowed the car and pulled up in front of a solid wood fence, weathered gray and overgrown with a vine of tiny pink flowers. The vine was tangled up with a climbing rose that was in bloom, too, and they grew together over an arch with a wooden gate under it. All together it looked like a postcard from my grandma's time.

Ma and I got out of the car. A grove of oak trees beyond the fence cast slight shadows over the garden. Beneath the oak trees were smaller, lacy-leafed trees and shrubs with leathery green leaves. The eave of a shingle roof jutted out above the shrubs, all but the edge of Vivian Bowers's house hidden in her garden.

Ma stood beside the gate and pulled on a short rope with a knot on the end. A bell rang on the other side of the fence.

"I think we can just go in. Vivian's expecting us."

Ma lifted a wooden latch on the gate and we let ourselves into the garden. We stood inside the gate for a moment on a wide fieldstone entry with low plants growing in the cracks between the stones.

It's hard to say what I experienced then—sound changed, quiet surrounded me, birds and water creating a calm hush. The air moved slowly over me, a cool current as if I were standing in a pool underwater.

"It's like going into a dark movie theater on a sunny day," Ma whispered.

"For me, too. My eyes need to adjust."

I walked ahead on a grass path that wound between shrub beds and then disappeared in front of me beyond clumps of rosebushes and many other flowers I couldn't name. We walked under low-branching trees that made a delicate ceiling over the garden. Birds were pecking on the grass in front of us until we startled them into the trees.

"Goodness gracious." Ma had her hand on the side of her face. She stopped and bent over to stick her nose in three different kinds of roses, and that's how she was, bent over, her face in a bunch of roses, when Vivian Bowers came trotting around from behind the flower bed, saying, "Welcome, welcome, dear hearts," in a high, shrill voice, her arms open wide to greet us.

Vivian's features were painted like an old-fashioned porcelain doll's, her face powdered chalk-white, thin eyebrow lines drawn on in a way that gave her an expression of constant surprise, each cheek dabbed with a deep pink dot. Her hair was dyed bright red and fixed in small pin curls that vibrated when she moved.

"That's 'Grand Duchess Charlotte'—don't you love it? This is 'Herbert Hoover,' more enjoyable as a rose than a president, just my opinion." Vivian laughed and gave "Herbert Hoover" a sniff, and with her thumb and forefinger snapped a spent flower off at the head. She held the petals in her hand, then dropped them in the pocket of her denim overalls.

"When I bought this house," Vivian said, "the closest thing to a garden was the floral-print drapes in the living room, and of course there were these oaks." She waved her hand. "I guess I bought the place for the oak trees." Ma strolled beside Vivian, and I followed behind, letting my hand drift over plants, feeling leaves and flowers, listening to Vivian chatter.

"Right here where we're standing it was bare, a vacant lot. Nothing but weeds. Can you imagine? After I bought it I came out here with a shovel and jumped on it with both feet. The darn shovel just bounced. I'm out here bouncing around thinking I'm going to make a garden. That was more than twenty years ago."

Vivian paused and turned around to look at me.

"I'll bet you're bored to tears, young man," she said. "Gene is out back." She pointed. "Right through there, that gravel path, go say hello to him. He'd love some company. Your mother and I have talking to do, gossip. Would you like some iced tea, Margaret?"

That's the way it was the first time I saw Gene Tole, Vivian and Ma going off for some iced tea and gossip and me left alone to wander around the garden. When I found Gene, he was working, digging potatoes in the back behind the laurel hedge where the vegetable garden was.

The afternoon sun shone bright and sweat made dark places on his plain white T-shirt, under his arms and down the center of his back. I stood in the opening of the hedge where the gravel path went and watched for a moment, shy to go into the vegetable garden and meet him.

This is how Gene worked. He moved along a row of potato plants, and near the base of a plant, he pushed a spading fork into the soil with his foot, rocked the handle of the fork back and forth, then bent over and with one hand on the stems of the potato plant and the other on the fork, he pulled and lifted the plant loose from the earth, potatoes dangling on the roots, dropping off into a lug box sitting there, or falling on the ground around it.

Gene stood up straight, put his hand under the waist of his shirt, and pulled his T-shirt up to wipe his face and forehead. He combed his blond hair back with his fingers, and looked over to where I was standing.

"Greetings," he called. "Come on in, don't want to miss any of the fun." He smiled wide and waved me into the vegetable garden.

Gene shoved the spade into the earth, gripped his left hand around the top of the handle and rested his right arm on top of it. He leaned on the spade, made his arm muscle show more.

"I'm Gene Tole," he said. He reached out and shook my hand. He shook my hand as if I were a grown-up, gripped my hand tight like that for a moment, made me feel like I was someone.

"My name is Dave," I said.

"Vivian told me you might come by this afternoon, you and your mother, to talk some more about building a garden."

"Yeah," I said, "that's us. We're here." I heard myself, sounded pretty stupid. "Ma's in the garden talking to Vivian." I gestured over my shoulder.

Gene turned back to the row of potatoes and started digging.

"How come you're digging potatoes?" I asked.

"Couple reasons," he said. "It's great sport. Beats fishing. You always turn up a great catch with not much effort, but then I've never been a big fisherman."

"I thought you studied horticulture."

"I did. Growing potatoes is horticulture. Ever hear of Luther Burbank?"

I shook my head.

"A famous horticulturist. He improved the Irish potato so much he practically invented it."

Gene held a plant out to me, heavy with potatoes.

"Shake the soil off these, will you?"

I took the plant and shook dirt from the potatoes, shook the potatoes off the roots and into the lug box.

"What's the other reason?" I asked.

"Other reason for what?"

"You said a couple reasons, for digging potatoes."

He stopped, looked at me a bit. "Dinner," he said. "What's dinner without a few potatoes?"

That was how Gene took me into his company, into the sport of digging potatoes.

We worked then in silence for a while. Gene spading, pulling, and handing the plants to me, expecting me to be there, to be his helper. I shook the dirt off, dropped the potatoes in the box, and tossed the plant aside onto a pile. We worked in a rhythm, digging potatoes, creating a harmony.

"That ought to do us," Gene said.

He pushed the spading fork into the soil and lifted the lug box and carried it to the gravel path, where there was a faucet and short hose. He sat on a wooden stool and began sorting through the potatoes in the lug box.

"Tell you what, there's a bucket over there under that apple tree." He pointed. "Let's wash a few of these little guys off for you and your ma to take home."

By the time I got back with the bucket, Gene had a pile of tiny red potatoes started.

"Pick out the ones about the size of a marble, none bigger than my thumb." He held his thumb out to compare. The tiny red potatoes made a plinking sound as they hit the metal bucket.

Gene stood up and turned the faucet on. He squirted water onto the potatoes, swirled the bucket around like he was panning for gold, poured the muddy water out, and kept squirting more in until the potatoes were clean.

"What good are they?" I said. "So little."

"They're the best for cooking. I'll tell you what you do. You take a cast-iron frying pan, put a chunk of butter in it— don't be shy with the butter. When it's melted, put the potatoes in. Shake the pan a bit. Spreads the butter on the potatoes, cooks them all over."

With his hand holding an imaginary fry pan, Gene made a slow circular motion in front of him.

"Cook them for five or six minutes. Poke the potatoes with a fork to be sure they're tender, sprinkle them with salt—not too much, just enough—and you'll have something better than candy to eat. You'll never go back to candy."

I said, "Okay," but I wasn't at all sure. Men in my family didn't cook anything. Dad never even made popcorn.

"How come you cook?" I asked.

"I enjoy it. I like to cook. And I'd starve if I didn't, nobody's going to cook for me."

"You live alone?"

"Right back there." He pointed to a small wooden building, low to the ground and hidden behind rows of berry bushes supported by wires and posts. Grapevines grew on an arbor that was part of the front porch.

"It's part of my pay," he said. "Just three rooms in a row, cozy."

He cleared his throat and ran his fingers through his hair.

"I talked to your mother on the telephone the other day about building a garden around her house. I understand you want to help," Gene said.

"She say that?"

"It's true, isn't it?" For a moment, Gene didn't say anything, just looked at me. "Building a garden is satisfying work. It's something we do now that'll be enjoyed in the future, maybe even after we're gone."

I picked up the bucket of tiny potatoes and played with them, cool and wet in my hand.

"It's the most optimistic thing I know to do. Especially planting trees. It's like teaching children."

"There are a lot of trees at the Home Place already," I said.

"What kinds? Do you know different kinds of trees?"

"I know oaks," I said, and sat the bucket down. "And walnuts, English walnuts and black walnuts."

"Are there walnuts at your ma's?"

"There's a black walnut out by the road," I said, "and on the ranch we had forty acres in English walnuts. I don't live on the ranch anymore."

"I see," Gene said.

By the way he said it, I knew my mother had told him about us, or maybe it was Vivian Bowers that told, but he knew. I was glad he knew, sorry at the same time. I looked away, my face hot, not just from the sun. My family had come apart; it felt to me like we had failed. I didn't know what to say or how to act anymore. I didn't even know what to think.

"Your mother asked me to draw a garden plan for where you're living now," Gene said. "I'll need to take some measurements. You going to be around tomorrow morning?"

There was a pause. We looked at each other.

"I'll need someone to help. Someone to hold the end of the measuring tape. Stuff like that. You going to be around?"

"Sure, I'll be there."

"Great. See you in the morning then, Ace." He shook my hand again and turned away.

I sat down and thought about being called Ace. Thought

of ace being number one, like in cards; ace being a crack fighter pilot.

The next day Gene Tole came to the Home Place and walked about looking at where the buildings were and at what was already growing there, which wasn't much. He made a sketch of the property and the house and where the tank house stood behind it. He drew the porches wrapped around three sides of the house and located the barn where my mother parked the car and where the valley oak trees grew and where the black locust trees grew, too, although Gene called the oaks Quercus and the locusts Robinia.

"*Quercus lobata, Robinia nigra*," he said. "Remember it."

I walked around with him, holding the end of his tape measure, and I tried to see my grandmother's house and land the way Gene was seeing it. Gene said how much he liked the shingle siding on my grandmother's house and how he liked the way the house was mostly two story, except in the rear, where it stepped down and the kitchen was only one story.

"The widow's walk is great," Gene said, "really sets the house off." He stood back from the house, taking it all in.

"What sets the house off?" I said.

"That little wrought-iron fence around the top of the roof," he said.

"You like that fence?" It reminded me of the family plot in the cemetery, but I didn't mention that.

"It's a nice detail," he said. "You don't see that sort of thing anymore. I like it."

To me the fence seemed pretty useless up there enclosing nothing, but if Gene Tole liked the widow's walk, I'd try rethinking my opinion of the thing.

When
You
Build
a Garden

 MY MOTHER HAD PROJECTS GOING
on all over the old house, inside and out. Ma used the money
she'd gotten from her mother to make the place more liv-
able, more ours. She hired a man to replace loose shingles on
the roof and paint the roof with linseed oil. The roof man
reset loose bricks in the chimney tops, moving around up
there like a widow in the widow's walk. Then he cleaned the
gutters. My mother hired a crew of five men to come wash
the house, scrape it, and paint it.

Inside the house my mother and I moved furniture.
Some furniture that my mother didn't want anymore we set
on the front porch for the Salvation Army. We painted
rooms and washed floors. My mother made new kitchen curtains and I hung them. We cleaned out closets, cupboards,

and the shelves on the back porch. My mother called the Salvation Army on the telephone and said, "Come and get it."

When the painters were done and had cleaned up their mess and moved their equipment out, the old house looked wonderful, looked like it had a fancy new party dress on, like Cinderella ready for the ball. The main portion of the house was painted a dusty rose color my mother called taupe; the trim was creamy white, and the porches were creamy white, too. Every few hours my mother would drop what she was doing in the house and go outside and walk around, looking at the house in its new paint job. I went along.

"Isn't it wonderful?"

"Sure is, Ma. Looks great."

"Makes everything else look worse, though."

She stood, her hands in fists propped on her waist, and kicked at a clump of thistle to scuff off the top.

"Makes this yard look absolutely Appalachian," she said. "Get that old mower out of the shed and see if you can make it run. Knock some of these weeds down. It'll help."

I got the mower to start with only five or six pulls on the rope, and set about mowing everything in sight around the old house. I went right up the to the brick foundation where it wasn't covered by privet bushes; where there were privet bushes, I pushed the mower under the bushes to get the weeds there and I mowed out in the open where foxtail, star thistle, and most every other weed you could imagine grew. A lot of what I mowed over was bare ground, dust and dirt flying everywhere so thick I could hardly see, like mowing in the eye of a dust devil, dust devil following me everywhere I mowed.

It was three hours later when I finished and put the mower back in the shed and went in the house to collect some praise from my mother. I walked into the kitchen and she just stared, started laughing at me, slapping the draining board with her hand, laughing so hard she couldn't make a sound, tears running down her face, staggering around the kitchen holding her stomach, me just standing there, her stomach still shaking when she finally sat down at the kitchen table and pulled herself together enough to wipe her eyes, blow her nose.

"Go look at yourself in the mirror," she said, started laughing some more.

I went into the front hall where a mirror hangs over a long narrow table and I saw what Ma had seen. I was completely covered with dirt. You couldn't make out my features; all that I could see were my blue eyes looking back at me, the white parts shining, and my lips, which I had been licking to keep from getting too dry. I had to laugh, too, and my teeth showed up bright and regular. My curly black hair looked like a fuzzy brown dust mop now.

"Sorry," Ma said. She stood behind me looking in the mirror, too, wiping her face on her sleeve. "You surprised me, that's all."

She put her hand on my shoulder, her arm resting on my neck. Then she lifted her hand and arm away, looked at them, and started wiping them on her apron. She laughed some more.

"Better shower," she said.

"No kidding," I said.

I went to the back porch to take my clothes off, then went up the back stairs two at a time in my Jockey shorts. It made me feel good to have knocked the weeds down, to have knocked a bit of the Appalachian out of the yard around the Home Place.

That night at dinner my mother said Gene Tole was coming over in a couple hours to show us the plan he had drawn for the garden around the old house. Ma was excited, and later when there was a knock on the door, she got up and turned the radio off during "The Voice of Firestone," her favorite program, where Renata Tebaldi was singing scenes from *La Traviata* at the top of her voice.

"Darn it," Ma said. But Gene Tole at the door won out over Renata Tebaldi on the radio.

Ma, Gene, and I went into the kitchen, where Ma poured coffee for Gene and herself. I got a Coke out of the icebox, popped the cap, and took a swig directly from the bottle. Gene spread the plan on the kitchen table. To keep the plan flat, he put the salt and pepper shakers on two corners, the sugar bowl on the third, and weighted the last one down with his coffee mug. He smoothed the plan out with his hand. It looked to me like he had scrubbed his fingernails— they were pretty clean for a gardener. He wore a new-looking khaki vest over a white shirt, and fresh black pants—Can't Bust 'Em's, with the gorilla emblem over the back pocket.

Gene explained to Ma and me what the plan meant and how the garden would be laid out, what it would look like when it was grown up, "when it matured," he said.

"The herb garden will be the most formal element in the landscape," he said. He pointed out the window above the table where we stood. "It will be a classic kitchen garden."

"To match our classic kitchen," I said. No one laughed. I decided to keep my humor to myself.

Gene talked about unifying factors and architectural elements to tie things together. He talked about plant textures, evergreen screens, perennial beds, and herbaceous borders. He talked about creating elevation changes, building a rock retaining wall, a terrace, a pergola, planting annuals and a cutting garden.

"Oh, yes," Ma said, "a cutting garden, that's great."

Gene talked about how flat the land was around my grandmother's house and how exciting and important elevation changes were in the landscape. Then he began to talk about the pit behind the shed where my mother parks the car. My grandmother's father had owned a brick company and he'd dug clay from there to make bricks. What my great-grandfather had left for us was a huge hole in the ground, a depression ten or twelve feet deep that covered almost three acres.

"It would make an incredible sunken garden," Gene said. He had one hand on the plan, fingers arched and spread, his other hand in the air, open, as if he held a precious imaginary world there in his palm.

"Don't you think that's a bit grandiose?" Ma said.

We all looked at one another—Gene, my mother, and me—and then we laughed.

"It's an idea," Gene said, both hands on the plan now, "something to think about."

But that word, *grandiose*, stuck with us and it became a joke while we were building the garden.

It was two days later, mid-morning, sunny, but not hot yet. A soft breeze was riffling the leaves in the tops of the oaks and locust.

I was sitting on the steps of the side porch absorbing the sunshine, thinking but not thinking, when Gene Tole came driving into the yard with his Studebaker pickup pulling a low trailer, a small tractor on it. The tractor had a scoop on the front and a chisel on the back.

Gene got out of the pickup and took his straw hat off the seat and put the hat on his head. Then he lifted the hat up, ran his fingers through his hair, and set the hat down on his head again.

"It's time to work on the foundation," he said.

"Foundation?" I said. I stood there for a moment thinking about the foundation.

"Maybe we better check with Ma first," I said. "I didn't know there was anything wrong with the foundation." I looked at the tractor.

Gene laughed. "Didn't mean to fool you," he said. He walked to the trailer and unhooked the chain that held the axles of the tractor to the trailer.

"Soil is the foundation of a garden; everything depends on it. Too many people forget the soil. If they don't see it, if it's not above the ground and blooming, they don't care. Big mistake."

I walked to the other side of the trailer and unhooked the chains that held the tractor on that side. Gene lifted a red five-gallon can of gasoline out of the pickup bed and poured fuel into the gas tank on the tractor. He returned the gas can and unlatched the clamp that held the trailer bed level on the metal frame. He took a key from his pocket, jumped up on the trailer and mounted the tractor, made me think of a rodeo cowboy.

Gene started the tractor, looked at me and motioned that I should stand back. He pushed the clutch, shifted gears, released the foot break, and the tractor rolled backward slowly. Gene looked down over his shoulder, watching the trailer bed. The front of the bed reared up, balanced a second like a teeter-totter, then the rear of the bed slammed to the ground.

The tractor bounced and Gene's straw hat flew into the air; his hand shot out to grab it, but missed. That was how I saw Gene Tole that morning—cowboy gardener. He backed the tractor the rest of the way off the trailer. I went around the trailer and picked up his straw hat, slapped it against my thigh to knock the dust off, and took it to the side of the tractor and handed it to him.

"Thanks, Ace." He grinned, placed the hat on his head, and tapped it with his hand.

He drove the tractor around to the west side of the house. I followed along behind on foot, sat on the kitchen steps and watched. Gene stood up on the tractor looking around, surveying the situation. He sat down, started the tractor rolling in first gear, engaged the power takeoff, and the chisel lowered into the hard soil.

Most of that morning I watched Gene drive the tractor back and forth, breaking up the ground. The tractor vibrated, jerked, and jostled Gene the whole time. He looked back over his shoulder to check how the chisel was doing. After he had broken up the dirt in one direction, he drove back and forth across it at a right angle to break it up some more. It was four in the afternoon when he parked the tractor by the side of the tank house. He got off, stretched, and said, "That ought to do it for now, ought to get us started anyway."

I walked with Gene around the house to where the Studebaker was parked. He unhitched the trailer and left it beside the driveway. When he was about to go, Gene stood leaning on the open door of the pickup, his arms folded across the top, the side of his head resting on his arms.

"We should have some sand, manure, and loam delivered here tomorrow morning," he said. "If they get here early, before I do, ask the drivers to dump out there beyond the tractor. Okay, Ace?" He made a lazy gesture with his arm.

"Sure," I said. "I'll do that."

Early in summer, after the sand, manure, and loam were spread, Gene Tole and I began to build the garden my mother wanted around her family home.

I was sitting on the tailgate of Gene's old, pale-green Studebaker pickup, swinging my legs back and forth while Gene rummaged around in the cab of the pickup saying, "I know it's in here somewhere." He thrashed about, sorting through the hand tools, the newspapers, the pipe fittings, the paper coffee cups, the rubber boots, and the nursery catalogs, part of what filled the floor and half the seat of the pickup.

"It's got to be here somewhere," Gene said. "Dammit anyway."

I turned around and through the rear window I saw the top of his shoulders, his powerful hand clenched on the back of the seat to steady himself. With his other hand, Gene fished around under the seat. The sound of glass clattering against metal drowned out his muttering. Gene straightened up, his back filling the window, and in his hand was the rolled-up plan he had drawn for Ma's garden.

"Got it," he said.

Gene came to the back of the pickup bed and stood beside me, facing me, his thighs pressed against the tailgate where I sat. He leaned into the pickup bed and tossed a shovel and rake forward against the cab. He grabbed a coil of garden hose and threw it to the front of the truck, too. He pulled a wheelbarrow that sat upside-down off the tailgate. With the palm of his hand Gene brushed dirt and sawdust from the pickup bed, then spread the roll of paper out on the tailgate. He weighted the corners down with bricks that were in the back of the truck.

I slid off the tailgate and stood beside him, both of us leaning over the plan and smoothing it with our hands.

"Sometimes when you build a garden," Gene said, "you build a gardener, too. Someone to care for the garden when it's done."

We looked at each other.

"That's you, Ace." Gene tapped my chest gently with his index finger.

If there was a ceremony when we began building the garden, that was it. That's all the ceremony there was, and that's what it was like. It was Gene Tole looking into my face, tapping my chest with his finger, and telling me he was going to teach me to be a gardener.

Gene rolled the garden plan up and handed it to me. He got a pencil off the dashboard of the Studebaker and put the pencil in the pocket of the gray suit vest he wore. We walked west away from the house into the open field. Beyond our fence line I could make out Mexican laborers hoeing weeds in the onion rows that were part of the Pasacco girls' truck farm. My mother had gone to grammar school with the

Pasacco girls, and even though they all had married names, my mother still called them the Pasacco girls. The Pasacco girls were older than my mother, and I can tell you one thing for sure: they hadn't been girls in a long time.

When we were out in the field, Gene took the rolled-up garden plan from me and turned to face the house. Bare ground and dry weeds stretched across the field before us all the way to the tank house.

"We'll plant a hedge along this side." Gene pointed with the rolled-up plan, waving it back and forth in front of him, the sleeves of his blue work shirt rolled up over his elbows, his gray vest flapping.

"Not a formal hedge," he said, and wiped his forehead on his rolled-up sleeve, "but a big, shaggy, unclipped hedge. A mix of evergreen trees and broadleaf shrubs that will give the garden a boundary, create privacy, but nothing you'll have to trim, Ace."

"Okay." I nodded, but I couldn't see it the way Gene seemed to be seeing it. He shoved his fists into his pants pockets, the rolled-up plan held under his arm, and we began to stroll around the house.

"The hedge will enclose the garden," he said. "Privacy is important. A garden needs a sense of protection, needs to feel like a world all its own." He looked at me. "You agree with that?"

"I don't know," I said. "I never thought much about it before now, I guess."

"Most gardens are made to be looked at from the outside,

they're all for show. But I believe a successful garden is designed to be enjoyed from the inside. From within. The garden is for the people who live in it, never mind the outside show."

We turned a corner, walking along the imaginary line of the hedge.

"The screen will have lower-growing plants here. We want people to have a glimpse of the house from the road, but that's enough. A hedge protects the inside, protects what's personal."

Gene and I strolled around the north side of the house, walking under the huge black walnut tree, sixty feet high and nearly as wide, that grew where the gravel driveway met Mariposa Road.

"My grandmother remembered when her father planted this tree. She was a little girl." I ran my hand along the deep fissured bark on the trunk.

"*Juglans nigra*," Gene said.

"What?"

"*Juglans nigra*. Black walnut. Say it."

"Black walnut." I was acting like Gracie Allen talking to George Burns.

"Wiseacre," Gene said. "Say *Juglans nigra*."

"*Juglans nigra*," I said.

Gene and I walked on around the house. We didn't talk. I pushed my hands into my pants pockets to be a little like Gene Tole.

Gene stopped and looked across the land. Then he

looked at the house awhile. He gazed at the house a long time. He was imagining the way the garden would look around it, I figured. Not the way the garden would look when we first finished building it, but the way it would look in twenty years, when the plants in the garden would be grown. I gazed off at the land, too, at the house, but what I saw was not the garden. What I saw was the weeds, the dead privet, the bare ground that Ma called Appalachian.

We walked along beside the pit where my grandfather's company dug clay for bricks, walked between the house and the tank house, over the brick pathway that connected them. Then we walked back to Gene's green Studebaker.

Gene leaned over the side of the pickup and pulled a galvanized bucket full of surveyors' stakes out of the truck bed. He took a tape measure from the bucket and handed the bucket to me. There was a short-handled hatchet in the bucket and a ball of chalk line.

"It doesn't look like we can put this off any longer, does it?" Gene said.

"Nope. Guess it doesn't."

"The first thing we do is lay out the paths and beds. The paths are the skeleton the garden is built on. The beds are the body, the muscle."

"What about lawn?"

"Just fat," he said.

Gene took another look at the plan he had drawn, ran his fingers over it, looked at the house, and then he started talking to himself.

That's how Gene laid out the garden, by carrying on a one-man conversation with himself; he gave himself directions, made calculations, mused out loud, considered, changed his mind, got in a couple of arguments. He drew marks on the ground with the heel of his boot, and dropped surveyors' stakes where he made the marks.

Then laying out the garden became a dance. Gene turned to me and bent to place a stake. I bowed to pick up the stake and bent to pound it. I turned, and Gene was side-stepping down the chalk line, sashaying along the line until he reached the end, where he turned to bow, holding a stake. I bowed to pick up the hatchet, and did a side-step along the line after him. He bowed in one direction, I in the other; we met over a stake, I pounded it in, Gene tied the chalk line to it. We walked side by side along the line to the other end and then side by side back again.

"Let's see now," Gene said, "about here. Start of the herb garden. Right here."

I took a stake from the bucket and drove it into the ground with the hatchet. Gene moved on, stringing the chalk line behind him.

"Another stake here." Gene kicked a mark into the dirt with the heel of his boot. While I was pounding the stake, Gene was pacing along parallel with the house, counting strides.

I was running, trying to keep up with him.

"Should be about here." He was back against the house, counting paces, multiplying by three.

"Couple more stakes. Twelve feet and thirty-two feet."
He marked a line with the heel of his boot.

Gene stood at the end of what he said was the herb garden. What he called the herb garden looked to me like a giant cat's cradle that some kid had strung together over broken-up ground.

"There'll be a bench here," he said, "with a pergola over it, along this end, a vine on the pergola, too."

Gene leaned over the pickup bed and pulled a large paper sack to the edge.

"Dolomite lime," he said, and jerked the string on the top of the sack to open it.

He balanced the sack on his hip while he walked and tipped the end of the sack so a fine line of dolomite trailed along the boundaries of the chalk line. Made me think of the little girl with the umbrella on the Morton salt box.

Nothing Gene did made sense until he sprinkled lime on the main bodies of the design, filling in the lines the string made. When Gene finished dusting the rectangle on the ground outside the kitchen windows, the rectangle looked like the British flag.

Gene tossed the empty sack into the back of the Studebaker and sat down on the tailgate. When he looked up he saw my mother watching out the kitchen window. Ma's hands were propped against her hips. She was wearing an apron and held a dish towel in one hand. Then she smiled and grasped her hands together over her head in a victory gesture; she lowered her hands and started clapping. Gene waved to my mother, then moved his hand in front of him in a way that said, Oh, it was nothing.

"There it is," he said.

I sat next to him on the tailgate, swinging my legs back and forth, our shoulders almost touching.

"Yep," I said, "there it is."

"And now all that's left is for you to spade it up. This is where the gardener comes in. That's you. You're the gardener."

Gene clamped his hand over my upper arm and acted like he was going to push me off the tailgate. But he didn't. I knew he wouldn't.

I sat for a moment more on the tailgate of Gene's pickup and thought about it. Thought about spading the herb garden, thought about planting the herbs in the herb garden someday soon, and I thought about becoming a gardener like Gene said I would, to care for the garden he and I were building.

I slipped my butt off the tailgate of the pickup and went around the house to where the walkway went from the back porch to the tank house to get a spade. Not much sense in trying to spade the herb garden without a spade, I thought.

I came around the house, spade in hand, and there was Gene Tole standing by the pickup, leaning his hip against the fender, resting his big upper arm along the top of the pickup bed, the heel of his hand supporting his head, talking to Ma.

Ma was standing close to Gene, not wearing her apron

now, not carrying a dish towel, but in a clean, floral-print housedress. It looked to me like Ma had combed her hair and put on fresh lipstick, put some rouge on her cheeks, too.

"I found a spade in the tank house," I said.

"Um," Gene Tole said. That's all he said, um. He turned back and looked right at Ma, hanging on to her every word.

"I thought it would be nice. Nothing special, just us." Ma looked at me. "Just the three of us. I thought it would be nice to get to know you better. We can talk gardening, if nothing else." She made a short nervous laugh, looked at her hands.

"Sure," Gene said. "I'd like that, too."

There may have been only three of us standing there, but I felt like a fifth wheel, like a lump on a log, like a fish out of water.

"Just thought it would be nice" went singing through my head in the most sarcastic voice—just like I wanted to be saying it out loud right now.

"Sound good to you, Ace," Gene said to me, "if I come for dinner on Saturday night with you and your mother?" He looked right at me.

"Sure," I said. "Sure. Sounds great." I pretty much meant it.

"Go ahead and spade it up, Ace," Gene said. "I'll be over with the plants tomorrow." Then he left.

Ma and I had lunch—egg salad sandwiches, bowls of

tomato soup—and after lunch I went out to where the herb garden would be and started to spade.

I stepped over the chalk line into the bed near where the arbor would be built. Walked to the end of the bed and pushed the spade into the ground with one foot, tipped the handle back and lifted the soil on the spade, turned the spade over and dropped the soil back to where it came from. Then I jammed the spade into the soil two or three times to break up the soil and mix it with the manure, sand, and loam. Stepping back a pace, I did the same thing, all the same movements, and I continued the motions along a row.

That's how I went into my trance, a daydream that was dream enough to fill several days even though it was a single afternoon.

My first thought was about spading and how it was like plowing. Plowing on the ranch in March when tule fog crept in and filled the valley, eased across the land from the Delta wetlands where tules—plants most people called cattails—grew, and I thought about a time when I was little and we drove across the islands, over bridges, along levies, across the lowlands. And on the river an ocean-going freighter as big as a factory, smokestacks and all, moved slow on its way to the port of Stockton and the freighter looked, from where we were below the levy, like it was on dry ground, navigating through a cornfield.

I went from there to being a merchant seaman signed on to the freighter traveling around the world, Singapore,

Yokohama, Pago Pago. I was off the ship then and on a beach with natives, Tahitians, and I was lying on white sand, propped up on one elbow, and native women were waiting on me, bringing me fruit to eat, and fish, and their bare breasts were brown and heavy, with dark pointed nipples like in *National Geographic,* and I had my shirt off and wore only white cutoff pants, the threads frayed around my knees.

Had myself a boner going at this point.

Men in huts along the edge of the beach where sand met the jungle were cleaning fish, and children ran around naked while the women cooked and I thought about my family, the family I had living there, the woman I laid with in bed, had sex with, and the men I fished with.

I was spading and breaking soil and dreaming and along the beach in Tahiti came Gene Tole, walking barefoot, white pants with frayed edges like mine, only his blond hair gleamed in the sun, parts bleached white, and gold hair on his arms and chest, and the dark islanders thought he was a god come to save them—from what I don't know. Gene and I walked along the beach together and then into the dark jungle, he the hero, me the sidekick.

That's where I was, in the jungle of Tahiti walking up the side of a volcano with Gene, when Ma called me in to supper.

"Come on in," she said. "Supper is about ready. Time to wash up."

"Be right there," I said.

Champagne

 SATURDAY NIGHT ROLLED AROUND and I wondered if I was in the right house when I walked through the dining room at the Home Place. Ma had washed and ironed a white tablecloth without stains on it, a tablecloth I couldn't remember seeing before. She had polished silver candlesticks and silver knives and forks and spoons and had set them on the table. My mother had cut some Queen Anne's lace and cornflowers from the field. She had cut some flowers from the pomegranate tree, bright orange waxy tubes with ruffled orange petals at the ends. These things she had arranged in a small crystal vase, which she put in the center of the table where she and I and Gene Tole were going to eat dinner.

I decided to get out of the house before I got into trouble

or drafted into work I wasn't interested in doing. I took a book out the front door onto the porch for a quiet read before Gene showed up.

I was out on the front porch, lying across the glider, barely gliding, reading *Madame Bovary*, when Ma came to the screen door.

"Come in here and taste this, will you?" she said.

"Sure," I said.

I excused myself from *Madame Bovary* and followed my mother through the front hall, toward the back part of the house to the kitchen.

I was pretty disappointed in *Madame Bovary*. Somehow I'd had the idea *Madame Bovary* was about illicit sex. I had been reading the damned thing for a week and I hadn't hit sex of any kind yet.

"Just taste the sauce," Ma said.

She handed me a spoonful, her hand cupped under the spoon as she moved it toward my mouth, mother-giving-child-cough-syrup style.

"Tastes great. What is it?"

"Chinese pork chops. I got the recipe from Betty Crocker, but then I changed it quite a bit, so thanks."

"What would Betty Crocker think? You changing her recipe like that and all."

"I don't give a damn what Betty Crocker thinks," Ma said.

"She's probably turning over in her grave right now, you changing her recipe and talking about her like that."

"I don't think she's dead," Ma said.

"That doesn't make it any better, after all," I said.

"I don't think she was ever alive."

"What?"

"She was never alive."

"And you expect us to eat her Chinese pork chops?"

"She's just a made-up personality," Ma said. "Now go back to your book. I'm sorry I even asked you in here. Now go on."

"I saw a movie called *The Man Who Never Was*. It was about this guy in World War Two who—"

"I'm not interested," Ma said. "Now go back to your book."

"Maybe Betty Crocker was like that guy," I said, "like the man who never was."

"I don't think so," Ma said. "Go on."

"Okay," I said, "if that's the way you feel about it."

There I was lying on the glider, not gliding at all, reading about how tough things were getting for poor Emma Bovary and feeling pretty sorry for her and a bit panicked at the way things were going, and her not even having had any sex, not so that I could tell anyhow. Things were coming down around her in a pretty hard way when Gene came driving up the gravel driveway in his Studebaker pickup, ready for dinner on Saturday night.

Gene came up onto the front porch, his hair still wet from the shower and his face ruddy from scrubbing. He had a blue dress shirt on with thin gray and maroon stripes. He wore a light gray suit vest, looked like new. I sat up in the glider, and he sat beside me and gave a push with his feet and we got started on a little glide.

"Your ma got dinner all set?" Gene said.

"Just about," I said.

I went to the front door, opened the screen door, and went into the front hall before hollering.

"Hey, Ma, Gene's here."

"Okay, I'll be right there."

Before you know it she was, too. Ma was right there in the doorway, pushing the screen door open with one foot. She wore a green, gray, and blue dress, the pattern like clouds with tiny stars sprinkled around; it showed off her long waist and legs, made her look even more beautiful than usual, I thought. I wanted to say, Ta-da, like a trumpet sound, but figured I better not.

Gene got up to open the screen door further for her. She was carrying a silver tray with a dark green, almost black, bottle on the tray and three glasses, prettiest glasses I ever saw. I never knew she had them. Ma set the tray on the little wicker table that was there on the front porch and told me to bring the wicker rocker over from around on the side porch, which is what I did.

When I got back my mother was sitting on the glider with Gene and she had him working his thumbs to get the cork off the bottle. Gene had his thumbs against the cork and he pried it back and forth, edging the cork closer to the end of the bottleneck. Ma sat ready, holding one of the glasses for when the cork came out. It did with a loud pop and Gene poured the first champagne into the slender glass my mother held, the glass no wider at any point than a silver dollar. Ma was laughing while she held the glass, like a kid with a sparkler on the Fourth of July.

The three of us stood up then on the front porch of the old house, each holding a slender glass filled with champagne. We looked at the glasses, watched the bubbles of pale gold champagne rising from the bottom.

"Here's to our garden." Ma held her glass out toward Gene and me and raised it. "To the future of our garden. May it grow lush and green, may it bloom, and bloom, and bloom," she said. "May it flourish and prosper."

"May we all flourish and prosper," Gene said. He held his glass up like my mother and they touched glasses, and I held up my glass, too, and touched theirs. Then we all took a sip of the champagne.

"May we bloom and bloom, too," I said.

Then everything was quiet and there was a big hole in the talk where I had dropped my words. I took another sip of champagne, though. It tasted wonderful. The champagne made the inside of my mouth puckery to my tongue when I moved it around. The champagne made bubbles in my throat and belly, just like it did in the long slender glass, and I began to think tonight was going to be a pretty good night after all.

Gene and Ma and I walked down the wide front steps off the porch. We walked along the new pea gravel path Gene and I had laid out earlier in the week. The gravel made soothing crunchy sounds as we walked on it. We walked along beside the west porch toward the herb garden, and to the west in the distance the sun was setting all burnt and orange around Mt. Diablo, and the few clouds that were there turned burnt orange, too. The undersides of the clouds were the color of gold.

Gene and Ma and I each walked into the herb garden on a different path. We came from different directions, each making crunchy sounds on the gravel paths as we came. It was strange what we did; we obeyed the design laid out on the land. We could have taken one big step over the row of tiny hedge plants that would someday enclose the herb garden—one big step over the six-inch-high boxwood hedge plants would have put us inside what Gene called the parterre. But we didn't do that. We honored the plan Gene had drawn and laid out on the ground, and we honored the work we had done and the vision of what the garden would become in the future.

We behaved like what we saw there was the herb garden as it would be in three years—five years maybe—and we strolled around the edged created by the boxwood hedge. We acknowledged the architecture of the herb garden and the three of us met again in the center of it still holding our champagne glasses. We clinked our champagne glasses together again. In silence this time. And we admired our work.

"Wait until they grow, fill in," Gene said. He squatted down, haunches on heels, balanced on the balls of his feet, and he ran his hand over the tiny boxwood plants.

Ma was pinching sprigs of rosemary plants that hadn't been out of the gallon cans and in the ground three days. She held her fingers to her nose, inhaling like she was about to float from the fragrance. She brushed her hand through the wiry stemmed flower heads of the English lavender.

"Oh my," she said. "I love it. I just love it."

Ma and Gene and I sat around the dinner table for a while talking before I got up to clear away the dinner dishes so Gene had a place to rest his arms and elbows. Gene could get away with things at the dinner table that I couldn't, things like elbows on the table.

Gene and my mother should have some time alone, I thought, to talk about what they might not talk about if I was there. I excused myself and went upstairs to my room to check in on Emma Bovary. Things had been looking bleak for Emma when I left her before dinner. She had only a few pages left to pull herself together, and the possibilities didn't look good to me.

I was lying on my bed reading about poor Emma Bovary at the last, after she had taken arsenic and wandered off to her bedroom to die, reading about her after she had gone to bed and suffered for five or six pages instead of dying, Emma Bovary's mouth all swollen, her tongue burnt, her tongue burnt so bad it was sticking out of her mouth, black. No one could understand her speaking with that burnt tongue, lying there like a galvanized corpse, until she ceased to exist; that's what Gustave Flaubert said, "like a galvanized corpse, until she ceased to exist."

That's when I wondered, after I had read the last page and closed the book, what Emma Bovary's story would have been like if she had told it herself. What if Emma Bovary had told her own story there from her deathbed, burnt tongue and all, and not had her story told by Gustave Flaubert, who not only looked in on Emma Bovary's life and mind, but on everybody else's, too? Flaubert looked in on everybody's thoughts, all at the same time, at different times, from the same place, from different places.

I think Emma Bovary would have had something different to tell us if she had been telling it all herself, in her own words, and I'm not just talking about the sex part that I managed to miss somehow, either.

The
Silent
Treatment

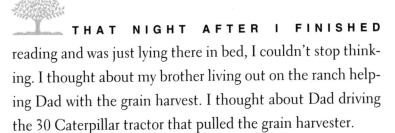 **THAT NIGHT AFTER I FINISHED**
reading and was just lying there in bed, I couldn't stop think-
ing. I thought about my brother living out on the ranch helping Dad with the grain harvest. I thought about Dad driving
the 30 Caterpillar tractor that pulled the grain harvester.

I thought about Gene Tole sitting at our dining-room
table, his big fingers and thumb holding the slender stem of
his champagne glass. Gene laughing, making me and Ma
laugh, too.

It was good to hear Ma laugh, a deep kind of laugh I
didn't remember from her before, and I was glad she had
Gene's company. I tried to be company for my mother, but I
wasn't adult company. Not yet. I barely had hair under my
arms. I didn't have any hair on my chest or face.

I lay there in bed and watched the moon move through the branches and twigs of the black locust tree outside my bedroom window. Sadness got right into my chest then and set up camp there. Sadness was lapping at my insides like waves on the edge of a lake. I didn't know how to calm myself, didn't even know what I was sad about.

What I thought about then was a special time with my father out on the ranch. It was November, a time when heavy frost covered the grass during the nights and in the mornings the grass and trees and the roofs, too, were white with frost and sparkled if the sun came through the fog.

This was a time when my brother, Brad, was sick with asthma and he couldn't breathe. Brad would wake up at night not able to get a breath and he had to sit up in a chair to sleep.

My family changed how we lived to make room for my brother's sickness. Ma stayed up all night with Brad; the bedroom became a hospital room, and the living room where Ma and Dad usually slept on a Hide-A-Bed was like a nurse's station. That's why Dad and I began sleeping in the bunkhouse.

"One Man's Family" was over and Dad turned the radio off. All the popcorn was eaten, butter and salt, all the old-maid kernels, too.

"Let's go, McCooge," Dad said to me. McCooge is what my father called me then.

"Where?"

"Out to the bunkhouse. We're going to be sleeping in the bunkhouse for a while."

"How come?"

"Make it easier on Ma and Brad. Make it easier on us, too," he said. He laughed.

"I don't want to," I said.

"Put on your pajamas," Dad said. "Bundle up your clothes so you can carry them out to the bunkhouse. You can dress yourself in the morning."

I put on my flannel pajamas—pictures of cowboys riding horses all over them—my wool jacket over the tops, rolled my clothes up in my pants, and put on my slippers to walk with Dad out to the bunkhouse.

Dad and I said good night and we left the house, all soft and warm, and walked outside into the clear dark night. We followed the dirt path, grass worn away from use, stepping around the puddles of water. Dad walked ahead and didn't notice at first when I stopped walking.

"What's the matter?" he said, looking back at me when he noticed.

"Sock in the mud." I started to cry.

"Sock in the mud?" He came back to where I was standing. "It's not a tragedy, little fella, a sock in the mud. You're a little Sock-in-the-Mud."

He tousled my hair and reached down to pick up my sock; he put my bundle of clothes under his arm. My father took hold of my hand then, and we walked on to the bunkhouse together like that, Dad holding my hand.

That is how I first touched my father that night. I held his hand as we walked from the house along the dirt path to the bunkhouse.

Dad had built a fire in the woodstove earlier that night to warm the bunkhouse, but it was still cold.

The bunkhouse had rough wood plank floors. A braided rag rug was on the floor beside the double bed.

Dad pulled down the covers on the bed and opened the sheets like an envelope for me to crawl into.

"I'll be right there. I'll help you warm up the sheets," he said.

Dad took off his clothes and hung them on nails along the wall. He quickly got into bed. He did not wear pajamas; Dad slept with nothing on. Even when it was cold, like it was that night, Dad didn't wear anything.

The bedsprings squeaked and grated metal against metal when Dad lay down in bed beside me. His weight held his side of the bed down, and I slid next to him. His body shivered a bit from the cold. I was turned away from Dad, facing the wall. Dad's body cupped me, and he put his arms around me, one arm under my shoulder, the other over my middle, and he cuddled me like that—made a nest for me with his body in the cold bed in the bunkhouse.

I felt the strength of Dad's arms around me, and I felt the softness of his chest when his muscles relaxed, and I felt the softness of his stomach when it relaxed, too.

"You like to snuggle up?" he asked.

"Yes."

"Your feet cold?"

"Yes."

"Rub them together like this."

Dad's legs moved a little and I could tell he was rubbing his feet together, and I rubbed my feet together, too.

The next morning when I woke up, Dad was gone. He had dressed quietly in the morning darkness, built up the fire in the woodstove to warm the bunkhouse for me, and he had spread my clothes over the wooden captain's chair and set the chair a few feet in front of the stove.

I put my clothes on and walked back to the house along the dirt path. The puddles were frozen. I picked up a stick and broke the ice on every puddle on my way to the house. Frost covered the grass and everything else and wasn't gone until half past noon that day.

I lay there in bed at the Home Place. What I was thinking was that I wished Gene Tole was my father. Not my father. How could I think such a thing? How could I wish it?

I got out of bed and stood by the window looking east for a while, looking at the moon getting smaller and more silvery as it rose higher in the sky, the moon still all tangled in the branches and twigs of the locust tree, and I ran my hand up and down the lace curtain, stroking the lace curtain by the window, liking the scratchy feeling.

Three feet below the window was the porch roof. I climbed through the window and stood on the roof, my back against the upstairs wall of the house. The heat from the day's sun still radiated off the tongue and groove siding. I pulled my T-shirt off over my head and wiped my face dry on it and blew my nose on it, too. I wadded up my T-shirt and threw it through the open window back into my bedroom.

I pulled the drawstring on my pajamas then and let my pajamas drop around my feet and I stepped out of them and stood naked a minute before folding my pajamas into a little pillow. I sat down, my naked butt sitting on the pajamas, my back propped against the wall of the house. My privates sitting on my pajamas, too, my privates feeling great, all comfy out in the open air, catching whatever breeze might blow by.

I began to imagine a story as I sat out there on the porch roof all nude. I imagined that an accident happened out on the ranch. I imagined my father driving the tractor pulling the harvester and my father jumped off the tractor for some reason—maybe he was attacked by a swarm of bees the harvester kicked up, that was it, he was attacked by a swarm of bees, and he jumped off the tractor while it was still running, and he rolled in the straw and dirt to get the bees off him, and as he rolled there in the straw and the dirt, the tractor ran over him and crushed him and he died out there in the field on the ranch.

The screen door on the front porch slammed and I could hear my mother and Gene walking on the porch and I could hear their voices.

"See ya Monday," Gene said.

"Take care."

"Thanks for dinner."

The screen door slammed again.

It was late, the moon high in the sky, free from the locust tree. Ma and Gene had talked a long time.

The engine of Gene's pickup started. The headlights came on. The headlight beams bobbed up and down as the pickup hit potholes in the gravel driveway. Gene stopped near the black walnut tree at the edge of Mariposa Road, then turned left toward Stockton. I watched the lights of the Studebaker pickup disappear around the curve of the road beyond the Pasacco girls' place.

After the headlights of Gene's pickup disappeared, I picked up my pajama bottoms and stepped through the open window back into my bedroom. I lay down on my bed in the hot summer night and thought about the rest of the story of me and Dad sleeping in the bunkhouse when my brother had asthma.

Dad was gone from around the house the next day, the day after he and I slept in the same bed in the bunkhouse, the day I broke the ice on all the mud puddles, the day the frost didn't leave until half past noon.

That evening Dad didn't talk when he came in to wash up or when he sat down at the supper table. That night at the supper table he kept his head down, didn't look at us, and only said the things he had to say to eat supper. Dad said, "Pass the potatoes" and "I don't want dessert." That's all he said.

That night when we sat around the radio, Dad didn't

laugh at Fibber McGee when Fibber McGee went to the hall closet to get his golf clubs. My father didn't laugh at Molly when she hollered, "Not the closet, McGee, not the closet." He didn't laugh during the two full minutes of crashing sounds when all the junk in Fibber McGee's closet emptied out into the hall, or when McGee said, "I remember, I left my clubs in the garage."

Dad didn't say anything during "Truth or Consequences." When "Truth or Consequences" was over, he said, "Time for bed."

He got up and started to leave for the bunkhouse without me, before I could put my pajamas on or wrap my clothes up to go out to the bunkhouse.

"Wait for me," I called.

But the screen door slammed. My father did not call me McCooge or Sock-in-the-Mud. He didn't hold my hand or tousle my hair.

By the time I said good night to Ma and Brad and got out the door, I could barely see my father in the starlight as he turned the corner at the end of the dirt path and climbed the bunkhouse steps and disappeared. I ran as fast as I could without tripping or dropping my bundle of clothes, to catch up with him, but I didn't.

When I got into the bunkhouse my father was stepping out of his long johns. He hung the long johns on a nail in the wall. I smelled the sweet summer smell of ripe apricots in the sun that was my father's smell. Dad stood facing away from me so I couldn't see him. He got into the double bed alone and turned toward the wall, away from me.

I took off my coat and slippers and put them on the captain's chair with my bundle of clothes for the next morning. I didn't say anything. I stood on the braided rag rug beside the double bed and waited for Dad to lift me into bed with him or help me crawl over him or in some way make room for me in the bed beside him.

"I made up the cot for you, over there," Dad said. He didn't roll over to look at me. I don't know how he knew I was standing there.

"Did I kick too much?"

"No."

"Grind my teeth?"

"Turn out the light and get into the goddamned cot."

There were other questions, but I didn't ask them.

The sheets on the cot were cold when I got into them. I rubbed my feet together to warm them up, but I didn't get warm, not before I fell asleep. When I woke up the next morning, I was still cold. Dad was gone, there was no fire built up in the woodstove. He had not spread my clothes out on the captain's chair and set it in front of the stove to get warm.

My father gave all of us the silent treatment. I don't know why he did, but it lasted for seventeen days, seventeen days and a lifetime. Dad shut me and Brad and Ma out of his life. Ma called what my father did "giving us the silent treatment." She called it "putting us in cold storage," called it "putting us in the deep freeze." That's what Dad did to us, starting that day; he gave us the silent treatment for seventeen days, and by the time it was over, it was never really over.

Maybe Brad didn't notice much, because he was sick with asthma. And Ma maybe didn't notice it right at first either; she was being the twenty-four-hour Florence Nightingale. But I was alone with Dad, and I noticed.

This is what I did the first day. I got on my bicycle and rode through the walnut orchard down to Little John Creek to check on how thick the ice was. I broke a hole at the edge of the ice and skipped the pieces of broken ice across the unbroken part. I got on the raft to see if I could move it away from the shore. But I couldn't. The raft was frozen in the water and to the bank.

I rode by bike across the rickety plank bridge over Little John Creek and out into the stubble field. I followed the tracks made in the dirt by the trucks that hauled grain away during harvest. I stopped at a giant oak tree and sat propped against the trunk for a while. I took out my pocketknife and whittled on the pithy flesh of an oak ball. I whittled an old Indian's face, but no one else would have known what it was.

From there I pedaled west through the stubble field toward the Moro place, where there was a windmill on our side of the fence. I broke the ice in the watering trough beside the windmill and then climbed the windmill. The rungs of the metal ladder up the windmill to the platform were cold. The cold hurt my hands.

From where I stood on the metal ladder I could see the whole world. There was no horizon. The foggy gray land disappeared into the white sky, the land faded, and the immense sky sucked up the edges. The world was deserted. Abandoned. Wind whipped through the windmill frame, and I turned back before I reached the top.

I rode my bike along the fence line between our place and the Moros'. I thought about crawling through the barbed wire fence and walking the mile and a half over to the Moro place, but I knew that would seem weird to Mr. and Mrs. Moro and to old Mrs. Moro, Mr. Moro's mother, who was from the Azores and didn't talk about anything other than her girlhood there and her trip to the United States to marry Mr. Moro's father, sight unseen. I wasn't up for that kind of visit. Christine, the youngest Moro girl, who I liked a lot—she was pretty and nice—had graduated Escalon High School and worked now as a bank teller in Stockton. She had her own car. She wouldn't be home.

I stood there beside the fence for a while, thinking about visiting the Moros, holding my bike between my legs, my legs spread wide apart, balancing the bike back and forth, catching the handlebars, the frame of the bike feeling good against my legs.

Then I got back on my bike and rode along the fence line some more, following the truck tracks in the dirt, crossing

Little John Creek on the big concrete pipe culvert my father had put in when the second rickety wooden bridge across Little John Creek got too rickety. I cut across the stubble field, headed back to the yard then, and came to the yard through the back part of the walnut orchard to where a tank house stood behind the house.

The ranch where we lived and that my father farmed was owned by a wealthy family, the Munters, who lived in San Francisco. The Munters came to the ranch every two or three years for their summer vacation and to try living like farmers for a month. On the second floor of the tank house the Munters kept a small apartment for sleeping.

I leaned my bike against the side of the tank house and climbed the stairs that wound around and up to the apartment door. It was unlocked. I knew it would be.

The door of the Munters' apartment opened into one big room with a long narrow room beside it. The big room had a couch that could be made into a bed. There was a sink with a water faucet that ran only cold water. Beside the sink on the drain board was an electric hot plate with two burners on stubby legs. In the cupboards were a few dishes and glasses and pots and pans.

The walls of the apartment were tongue and groove siding painted yellow, the color of butter. It was cold in the apartment, the air was damp and stale, and I felt like an intruder even though no one was living there. The air smelled of stale cigars; maybe old Mr. Munter smoked when he was alone. In their apartment, the Munters had extras of things we didn't even own; for one thing, they had a wind-up phonograph. They had a bunch of records, too. Some of the records were popular records. I recognized names from listening to the radio. There was "Goodnight, Irene" by the Weavers, and "Mañana" by Peggy Lee. There were opera records in three-record volumes with a story of the opera to go with it. There was a record of highlights from *The Student Prince* by Sigmund Romberg. There were several records by Billie Holiday. I had never heard of Billie Holiday. At first I thought Billie Holiday was a man, then I saw a picture on the back of a record jacket and saw that she was a woman, a Negro woman at that. The Billie Holiday records belonged to Tim Munter, old Mr. Munter's grandson, no doubt; no one else in that family would listen to records by a Negro woman.

There were books in the apartment, too, reading books and picture books of places to travel to and of art in famous museums. I took a large flat picture book off the shelf and sat down on the couch and looked at the paintings in the book for a while. The paintings were in a palace somewhere in Spain. Some pictures were of the palace itself; the pictures I liked most were of a courtyard in the palace. The courtyard had fancy arches and tiles and a fountain in the center that rested on the backs of stone lions, and water ran from the fountain in four directions along small channels.

I closed the book and put it back on the shelf where it had been. In the smaller room of the Munters' apartment were two bunk beds built right into the wall. They stuck out like shelves, and that's what old Mr. Munter called them, the sleeping shelves. I climbed up the ladder, which was built into the wall, too, and lay down on the top sleeping shelf. The mattress smelled musty, made me think of damp newspapers. I unfolded an army blanket from the foot of the bunk and pulled it up over me. I punched up a pillow, with no pillowcase, to rest my head on, and I began to think about Dad.

What I thought about was how few times there had been when Dad held me the way he held me the night we slept in the same bed in the bunkhouse. There was only one other time when he held me like that time in the bunkhouse, or even touched me, that I could remember. And there was only one time I could remember seeing my father cry.

The time my father held me was a time when we were at Woodward Reservoir swimming and having a picnic. We ate roast beef sandwiches that Ma had made with mayonnaise, mustard, and sweet pickle relish. That's how my mother made roast beef sandwiches, with sweet pickle relish. We ate potato chips and drank iced tea from the thermos and lemonade from the refrigerator jar.

My mother and father and Brad and I had been swimming, and now Ma and Dad sat on a blanket beside the car, parked in the shade of a junk willow tree at the edge of Woodward Reservoir. Ma called to Brad and me where we played in the mud of the shallow water. Brad and I were playing in the reeds, squeezing the jelly sacs of frog eggs that hung suspended from the reeds. Ma called us to come eat watermelon.

The four of us were eating watermelon when a man a little ways away from us started hollering and waving.

"Isn't that Bill Tull?" Ma said.

"Looks like him," Dad said.

We knew the Tulls slightly. Brad was a grade behind Shirley Tull at Collegeville School. The Tulls lived in Collegeville, but we didn't associate with them. They were a large family living in a makeshift house that Dad said made a chicken coop look good. Dad called the Tulls Oakies.

Mr. Tull ran into the water and began swimming out to the diving platform, where my brother and I weren't allowed to go because we were too young. More people came from beyond where the Tulls' car was parked and they were yelling and waving, too. Dad jumped up then, and he ran toward the water in his swimming trunks with swordfish on them, and Ma got up and started running toward the diving platform, and Brad and I ran ahead of her, after our father.

High-school boys were diving off the platform and going under it. Finally they came out with something, and I knew it must be a person. Mr. Tull was at the platform then, and he began to swim back to shore using one arm, his legs kicking hard; his other arm cradled a head against his side. Thick red hair washed over Mr. Tull's arm.

It took Mr. Tull a long time to get near the shore. When he could reach the bottom, he ran through the water holding a boy in his arms, hugging the boy to his chest as he came out of the water. It was Willie Tull. Mr. Tull put Willie down quickly on a blanket and pushed on Willie's chest and then let up. Mr. Tull pushed again and let up again. More people gathered quietly around Mr. Tull and Willie. There was no sound. Green slimy water came from Willie's mouth when Mr. Tull pushed down. When he rolled back on his knees and released the pressure on Willie's chest, Mr. Tull threw his head back and moaned.

It was then that Dad put his hands on my sides, under my armpits, and he lifted me up, turning me around toward him, and he held me against his naked chest, gently. Dad's forearm was under my fanny, the fingers of his other hand cupping my head against the soft part of his neck and shoulder, and he held my head there gently so I couldn't see the boy who drowned or his father, who rocked over him.

I got cold lying on the sleeping shelf, army blanket or not, and jumped down and went into the big room that was the main part of the Munters' apartment, where there was an electric heater. I plugged the heater in and propped myself on the couch in front of it and waited to get toasty. The heater was a copper bowl on a short stand; wires circling a ceramic cone in the center of the copper bowl turned red and gave off warmth. The heater hummed and filled the room with the smell of burning dust.

The first record I played was "Goodnight, Irene" by the Weavers. Only a couple of years ago you couldn't turn on the radio without hearing it, but now I didn't hear it nearly enough. I wound up the Victrola and moved the needle arm over the record and set the needle in the record groove and played the record over and over.

In "Goodnight, Irene" the Weavers tell the story of a man who is married to this woman, Irene, for only a week, since last Saturday night to be exact. The man loves Irene a lot, but he goes downtown to gamble anyway, and Irene runs off and leaves him. The poor guy who sings the song—well, it's really the Weavers singing the song for him—says at the end, "Sometimes I have a great notion to jump into the river and drown." It's really a pretty sad song, and I started feeling better just listening to this guy's troubles.

And as though that wasn't making me feel good enough, next I put on this record by Billie Holiday, who was new to me, called "I'll Never Be the Same." The music started out all light and danceable, with a piano playing sweet and some horns blowing soft and a nice drum keeping the beat, and then Billie Holiday comes in singing about this louse she loved and how much wrong he had done her and how bad she felt and how she didn't know if it was worth it to go on living anymore. At the end of the song Billie Holiday said of course she would go on with her life, even though—as she put it—songbirds told lies and she wouldn't believe the skies, and her life would never be the same.

That's what she said, and as I looked back on it now, lying in bed the night of our dinner with Gene Tole, I knew the feeling she was singing about. I started thinking about my father again.

I thought about the time I saw my father cry. That time was the beginning of the trouble that came between Ma and Dad and made them decide to live apart.

It was fall, after the harvest was in. October, I guess. Late-afternoon shadows slanted from across the sky and fell stark on the gravel pad in front of the barn. The shadows distorted the shape of the barn, making it look like it was leaning way over. I had a stick and was drawing a line in the gravel that outlined the shadow shape of the barn.

Inside the barn my father stood holding the wheel of the John Deere tractor, spokes and hub painted yellow, propped against his leg and chest. My father bent over and with three fingers of his hand scooped amber-colored grease from a grease bucket and stuffed the grease into the hub of the John Deere wheel.

I looked up and saw Malcolm Minahan driving along the gravel road into our place, driving in his Buick Roadmaster with chrome portholes along the sides, driving around the knoll past the windmill, past what remained of the vegetable garden. My father looked up, too, still standing, holding the wheel propped against him, his fingers, covered with grease, stopped midair. My father looked out the big wide-open front doors of the barn.

Malcolm Minahan worked at Farmer's and Merchant's Bank in Stockton; he was one of the people at Farmer's and Merchant's Bank with his own office. Malcolm Minahan drove around the county stopping to talk to people and find out their news. This afternoon he didn't even get out of his Buick Roadmaster. He stopped right in front of the doors to the shop, after driving over my shadow outline. He rolled down the window of the Roadmaster and waited for my father to come out of the shop and talk to him.

My father took his time wiping the grease from his hands. He tossed the grease rag onto the workbench and walked out to hear whatever gossip Mr. Minahan had to spread that day. I stood beside my father and leaned against Mr. Minahan's Roadmaster, like my father did. The difference was, my father had to bend down at the waist to see in the Roadmaster window, and I could barely see over the window edge where Mr. Minahan rested his arm.

Malcolm Minahan's hand looked soft and pale; his fingernails were polished and he wore a big gold ring with a diamond in it. Biggest diamond I ever saw. I ran my pointer finger around a chrome porthole on the Roadmaster. The portholes were just for looks, didn't connect to anything.

Malcolm Minahan said a couple of quick things about the weather and the crops, then he got to the reason for his visit.

"Hear about the Moro girl?" he said.

"Which one?" Dad said.

"Teresa. Next to the youngest."

"No. What about her?" Dad's voice came out uneven.

"Committed suicide. Committed suicide this morning."

There was a long silence when my father just stared at Mr. Minahan.

"What's suicide?" I said after a while, but no one heard me.

"Jesus Christ." Dad stepped back from the Buick and looked down at his work boots. He looked at Malcolm for a moment, then he looked over at the walnut orchard.

"Did she leave a note?" Dad asked. He looked again at Malcolm Minahan.

"I guess Marie took the other girls over to Tracy to visit some Portagee friends of hers over there. Joe was hauling a load of seed over to Burnham Station. While they were gone, Teresa got Joe's rifle and shot herself in the head. Sat right there in the living room and shot herself, beautiful young girl like that, with everything to live for. I don't understand it. Didn't die right away either, I guess. Joe said she left a trail from the living room to their bedroom, Joe and Marie's, where Joe found her after he got back from Burnham Station. Found her lying there on top of the bed. Made quite a mess, I guess. Joe called Francis at the bank— that's how I heard about it—to go get Christine over at her Portagee friends in Tracy."

"Did she leave a note?" Dad asked.

"No. No note," Malcolm said.

Dad straightened up then and looked over the top of Mr. Minahan's car, my father's body blocking the window where Malcolm had been looking out. Dad stood that way for a while looking out across where the vegetable garden was, past the windmill and the fruit trees, across Jack Tone

Road to where Fred Ladd's hay barn used to be before it burned down.

My father didn't talk anymore to Malcolm Minahan. Dad pushed himself away from the Buick Roadmaster and hit the roof of the car with the heel of his hand, and he turned around and walked back into the shop.

Malcolm hollered, "Catch you later," and drove back out the gravel road to Jack Tone Road, a trail of dust following him along our driveway. The Buick Roadmaster turned toward Silva's place, the next ranch down Jack Tone Road, where Malcolm Minahan would retell the story of Teresa Moro's suicide.

When I went back into the shop, planning to ask my father again what suicide was—even though by this time I knew but couldn't understand—he wasn't there. I looked all around. He wasn't there.

I went out the back door of the shop to find him. It was the only other door. There was nothing on the back side of the shop but junk, scraps of metal, a lumber pile, pieces of old equipment we didn't use anymore, broken machinery, and the dead weeds that grew between it all.

Then I saw him. I saw my father sitting in the cab of the old Rio truck that had no doors, was built with no doors, that had hard rubber tires, had dead grass hanging in cracks in the wooden bed, grass waving in the breeze.

I walked along the back side of the shop and along the tractor shed, where my father wouldn't see me. I came up behind the Rio truck. He was sobbing. I heard Dad sobbing there in the cab of the Rio truck, where he sat with his head on the wooden steering wheel, his shoulders heaving up and down and Dad crying, "Oh God, oh God," every once in a while. And I knew my dad didn't even believe in God.

I couldn't think what to do then. I wanted to go around to the cab of the Rio truck and climb up on the running board, get in the cab and sit next to Dad and put my arms around his neck. But I couldn't do that with Dad in the best of times, which this wasn't. This wasn't the best of times. But right now it seemed even more important to me to put my arms around Dad. More important, more impossible.

Dreaming on the Road to Santa Rosa

 WHEN I CAME DOWNSTAIRS THE
morning after Gene Tole had dinner with us, my mother
said, "Would you like some French toast for breakfast?"

"Sure," I said, "sounds great."

"I already made the batter," Ma said.

My mother had been up for a while, I guess. The dishes
from last night's dinner were all done. The pots and pans
were done, too. The kitchen was spotless, and I knew Betty
Crocker would have been proud of us if she had ever been
alive.

"Extra cinnamon?" Ma said.

"Sure," I said.

Ma set a plate with four slices of French toast on the
table in front of me. Extra cinnamon on top and powdered

sugar, too. She had three strips of bacon lined up alongside the slices of toast. Ma took a small pitcher of syrup out of a saucepan on the stove where she had been keeping it warm.

"Don't you think Gene Tole is a nice-looking man?" Ma said.

"I don't know. I never paid much attention," I said. But that was a lie. I had paid attention to Gene's looks, and I thought he was a real nice-looking man. He was a handsome man. What I liked most about the way Gene looked was that even though he was blond, with sun-bleached streaks in his hair, his eyebrows were dark brown. It was striking, the color of his hair and the color of his eyebrows. But Gene didn't act like he was good-looking.

Gene's thick forearms were covered with blond and white hair, too, hair bleached white by the sun. When Gene wore a loose-fitting shirt you could see thick dark hair the color of his eyebrows that came to his neck and was kept back by shaving.

"Do you like Gene Tole, Ma?" I said.

"Oh sure, I like him," my mother said, "but nothing special. I enjoy his company—I enjoy his company a lot. Last night was great fun. Good laughs."

My mother poured more coffee for herself, in a thick white coffee mug, and sat down at the table with me. We both looked out the kitchen window toward the herb garden, admiring our work, checking to see if the plants had grown.

"Gene isn't the kind of man that would ever be interested in me," Ma said. She was thoughtful and sounded a little sad.

"What kind of man wouldn't be interested in you, Ma? You're beautiful, I think you're really beautiful."

Ma looked down at the table, fiddled with her coffee mug.

"It's more complicated than that."

"You think he's too young?"

"He is too young, but it's much more. You'll understand when you're older."

I was thinking then about how I wished I looked like Gene looked. I wished I had straight, thick, blond hair like Gene.

"Last night after you went up to bed Gene was talking about himself, talking about gardening and how he became a gardener. He said he got started by mowing the neighbors' lawns when he was a boy. He worked for Vivian Bowers in her garden and then worked for her over at the nursery. He went to Cal Poly in San Luis to study horticulture, then applied to work and study at a famous garden in England called Kew, he said. He worked and studied at Kew for a couple years."

My mother was still looking out the window at the beginnings of our garden. Then she turned and looked at me.

"The upshot of all this is that someone Gene knew at Kew Gardens is the curator of Luther Burbank's garden in Santa Rosa now.

"Luther Burbank who invented the Irish potato?" I said.

"Well," my mother said, "he worked on the Irish potato,

made it a whole lot better, but I don't think I'd say he invented it. Anyway, he hybridized the Burbank rose, the Shasta daisy, and a bunch of other plants. Luther Burbank is to plants what Thomas Edison is to the lightbulb."

"Oh," I said.

"Gene is going down to Santa Rosa this Thursday to visit his friend from Kew. He asked if I thought you'd like to go along for the ride, and to see Luther Burbank's garden, I guess. I said you probably would. You should think about it. It's fine with me, if you want," Ma said.

"I'll think about it," I said.

I got up to go outside and water the trees I had planted the week before. I wanted to think about riding with Gene to Santa Rosa and seeing Luther Burbank's garden and meeting Gene's friend from Kew Gardens, in England, and I didn't want my mother to see how excited I was to be asked to go on a trip with Gene Tole.

I went outside to water, and what I did was daydream. That's what I was doing that morning when I met Parkie, watering and daydreaming. The daydream part was like this: Gene Tole and me, in his old green Studebaker pickup, the pickup all shiny and clean in the daydream, gliding along smooth on Highway 4, across the islands through the Delta where the San Joaquin and Sacramento Rivers come together, heading toward Fairfield, where we would connect with the Black Point Cut-off, sailing along the north side of San Francisco Bay then, that part of San Francisco Bay called San Pablo

Bay really, the sun shining through the sparkling windshield, no spiderweb crack in the windshield now, cool Mediterranean breeze blowing on our faces from across San Pablo Bay, the breeze pushing up big puffy white clouds, Gene turning to look at me, just like Batman looks at Robin in the comics, and saying, "I know a place that makes great burgers, chocolate shakes out of this world," and by this time I'm tasting hamburger meat off a broiler and sliced red onion and tomato, lettuce, mayonnaise, and ketchup, no mustard, please, and thank you.

Then I hear this remark, "What you building, a pitch 'n' putt?" It's a fat kid in a dirty white T-shirt standing in front of me, staring. A kid about my age, a little older maybe, standing there where he walked off the shoulder of Mariposa Road, watching me water. The kid who turned out to be Parkie, only I didn't know it was Parkie at the time.

I just looked at him.

"You know, a pitch 'n' putt, a miniature golf course? What you need is a Dutch windmill with blades that go around like this." The kid who turned out to be Parkie gave a demonstration of what a Dutch windmill should be like with his arm.

"I saw a pitch 'n' putt up in Sacramento once," the Parkie kid said. "They had a whale, its mouth wide open, and you knocked the ball into the whale's mouth and the ball came out the top like the whale was spouting water. It was really cool. That's what you need here."

"Sure," I said, "that's just what we need."

"No kidding. That's what you need here all right," he said. "What are you building here, anyway?"

"A garden," I said.

"No kidding? A garden? I don't see any vegetables," he said.

"It's not a vegetable garden," I said. "Maybe that's why you don't see any vegetables."

"Don't be so touchy," the Parkie kid said. "You could make money with vegetables, or save money at least. No kidding. You could make a lot of money with a pitch 'n' putt. My name's Dexter Parkinson," the kid said. Like I should be impressed and start calling him Dexter Parkinson right off. He had his hand out to me at this point, all ready to shake. I shifted the water hose to my left hand, took a quick wipe on my Levi's with the right, and shook his hand. I decided right then I'd call him Parkie, if I called him anything.

"I'm a sophomore at Franklin," Parkie said. "You going to Franklin? I'm the youngest in my family. I have four older brothers and sisters—four in all, not each—and my mother and father thought they were done having kids, until I came along. I'm an accident. My brothers and sisters call me 'the accident,' or sometimes 'the mistake.' They say I'm spoiled, but what do they care, they're all married and moved out. No kidding. Except Geneva. Geneva is the youngest. Except for me. I'm younger. She's at home and she lets me drive her car once in a while, if I'm nice to her, and that's not easy. She's a bitch. No kidding. But sometimes she lets me take her car to the movies; mostly on Sunday nights she let me use it. I'll take you to the movies sometime," Parkie said. "No kidding. You want to go?"

"Well, maybe. Sometime," I said.

I took a good look at Parkie. He was a mess. Parkie had boobs any girl our age would have killed for. His T-shirt bulged and rolled and had dirty smudges where the bulges and rolls rubbed against everything Parkie came near. Parkie talked on like a stuck record player. He was a mess. I should have known right then he would turn out to be just about the only friend I had that whole summer.

This is how excited I was about going to see Luther Burbank's garden with Gene Tole. I was excited enough to ask my mother if I could get some new clothes.

"Hey, Ma," I said, "can we go downtown and get me some new clothes?"

"Sure," my mother said, "we can do that. You'll need new clothes for school when it starts anyway. That's only two months away."

"It's two and a half months away," I said. "Let's not rush it, okay?" I liked school, but this was a new school for me, with new kids, except for Parkie, and I had doubts about Parkie; he wasn't exactly a plus in getting started at a new school.

The next day, my mother and I went downtown to JC Penney's department store on Main Street in Stockton. My mother parked her big old Packard in front of the Ritz Theater, just down the street from JCPenney's. The front of the

Ritz Theater had glass windows for posters of movies that were "now playing" and movies that were "coming soon." *Red River*, with John Wayne and Montgomery Clift was coming soon. The poster in the glass window had a blue paper ribbon diagonally across the bottom that said, "BACK BY POPULAR DEMAND." I wanted to see *Red River*, but didn't say anything.

The ticket booth for the Ritz Theater was made to look like a silver shell, all scrolly and ornate, and it stuck out to the sidewalk right under the marquee. I felt sorry for the young woman who sat out there alone in the scrolly shell selling tickets.

The things I got at JCPenney's were a madras shirt, bright red, yellow, and blue woven together to make other colors; a new pair of Levi's, dark blue, stiff from being new; and a new pair of Keds, black high-tops, with a cream-colored rubber emblem saying KEDS on the side. My new Keds made my feet feel light when I put them on. They made me want to run and jump.

That's how I was dressed the morning Gene was to stop at the Home Place to pick me up to go to Santa Rosa and visit Luther Burbank's garden. I'd been up for hours, dressed in my stiff new Levi's with the cuffs turned up, the light-blue inside color showing on the outside, cuffs turned up so when my mother washed the Levi's they wouldn't end up too short, the leather patch saying LEVI'S sewn on where my belt covered most of it still soft and shiny, not dried and cracked from washing and hanging on the line to dry. New

Keds with the rubber emblem showing below the Levi's cuffs. Blue Levi's matching the blue in my new madras shirt. I was ready; I waited for Gene.

That morning as I shoveled Wheaties into my mouth, my mother got up from the breakfast table where she was drinking coffee from her thick white mug. She went to the cupboard and took an Ovaltine jar from the shelf. She unscrewed the lid on the Ovaltine jar and took several bills out. She separated one bill and put the others back.

Ma folded the bill over several times until it was a small square when she got back to the breakfast table.

"Here, you might need this for something," my mother said. She handed me the folded bill as she sat down.

"Oh, Ma," I said, "you don't need to do that." My face felt hot. Money was more personal in my family than sex, and sex was damn personal.

"Take it," my mother said. "You can never tell. You might need to buy something, get something to eat. You might want to give Gene some money for gas."

I unfolded the bill. It was a ten-dollar bill.

"This is way too much, Ma," I said.

"It's okay," my mother said. "You should have plenty, just in case. You've been working hard on the garden. You've earned it. Take it."

My face felt really hot. I looked down at the table and folded the ten-dollar bill back up like my mother had folded it, creasing it hard between my fingernail and thumbnail. It was quiet in the kitchen. I stood up and turned away from my mother so she wouldn't see how I felt taking money from her. I put the ten-dollar bill in the little watch pocket that was above the right front pocket in my new Levi's. I decided I'd keep the money there and give it back to my mother when I came home.

After breakfast I watched for Gene Tole's pickup through the front room window. Pretty soon Gene came driving along Mariposa Road, slowed down, and turned into our gravel driveway, drove past the black walnut tree and up to the house.

"See ya, Ma," I hollered as I ran down the front porch steps to get into Gene's pickup.

Gene got out of the pickup, standing with one foot on the gravel driveway, the other on the floorboard of the pickup cab. He rested his arms on the top of the open door. Gene had cleaned out the mess in the pickup cab—no bottles, tools, papers, pipe fittings. The dirt swept out, too.

Gene had a new shirt on, I could tell, and what looked to be a new vest—deep, dark red, the color of wine.

"It'll probably be late when we get back," he said to my mother, who'd come out to the porch. "If it looks like we'll be *real* late, I'll call."

My mother stood on the front porch and waved as Gene and I drove out the driveway. Gene turned left onto Mariposa Road. He honked the horn a couple times, bouncing the heel of his hand on the plastic knob in the center of the steering wheel. I looked out the back window. My mother had gone inside already.

I turned around and reared my butt off the seat to pull my new Levi's pant legs down to get comfortable. I propped my elbow on the open window, rested my other arm across the seat back.

We went through Stockton, but didn't take Route 4 like I had imagined we would. Gene drove north on the Lower Sacramento Road, past the Eight Mile Road toward Lodi. We came to Route 12 before we got to Lodi, turned left onto Route 12, and headed west toward Rio Vista.

Morning sunshine was behind us, shining on my shoulders through the rear window of Gene's pickup. We had the road to ourselves, passed a few farmers now and then, that was all.

Gene was quiet, so was I—Gene in his world of thought and me in mine, I guess, neither of us needing to break into the other's world to talk. The morning sunlight warm on my shoulders, Gene Tole's company warm on me all over. Gene's world of thought and my world of thought separate, unspoken, but overlapping there in the cab of the pickup headed for Rio Vista, headed for Santa Rosa, Luther Burbank's garden.

Mostly that's what I was thinking about—Luther Burbank's garden and what it would look like. The picture I had of Luther Burbank's garden was like the pictures of gardens I had seen in my mother's garden books. I imagined sweeping grassy lawns, maybe a pond, wide flower beds thick with annuals and perennials. I imagined shrubs, spreading shade trees, brick walkways, stone walls and terraces.

I thought, too, about Gene's friend Christopher Rudd from England, the horticulturist at Luther Burbank's garden. I thought about what he might be like. I had never met anyone from England before. Christopher Rudd was probably like everyone else, I decided, probably said "Greetings" when he met folks like Gene did, even if Gene wasn't from England and had lived there only awhile.

My father didn't have any friends like Gene had. My father was friendly with the neighbor men, with other farmers. But being friendly was different from being friends like Gene was, driving all the way to Santa Rosa to see his friend. My father's best friend was probably his brother Martin, my uncle Martin, who lived twenty miles away in Linden. Uncle Martin was probably my father's best friend, but every once in a while they cussed at each other and then didn't talk for a while—sometimes for years.

My brother was my best friend. But I didn't see him anymore since my ma and dad separated. I wondered what Brad was doing right now. This very minute. Here I was riding to Santa Rosa on a trip alone with a grown-up and Brad didn't even know I was doing it. Wait until I told him I'd been to Santa Rosa. Maybe Brad had gone somewhere special, too, and I didn't know about it.

Gene shifted the Studebaker pickup down as we crossed the Sacramento River on the Rio Vista Bridge. He slowed down so we could get a good long look at the river. What we saw was the river all broad and slow and sparkling in the sunshine, willow trees and poplars growing on the banks of the river, and Negroes fishing along the edge of the river where the water met the levee, their cars, old and junky, parked above the river beside the levee road.

"Are you hungry yet?" Gene asked as we drove slowly through Rio Vista. "Thirsty? Need to piss?"

"No," I said, "I'm fine."

"I'd like to get to Santa Rosa before noon," he said. "We're not halfway there yet." He didn't sound in a hurry, though.

Outside Rio Vista we picked up speed. We passed an old cemetery on the right with tall dark green trees that grew in narrow columns.

"Look at those trees," I said.

"Italian cypress," Gene said. "*Cupressus sempervirens.*"

"Oh," I said.

"*Sempervirens* means evergreen in Latin. Any plant with that name tacked on it is going to be an evergreen. Got it?" he said.

"Sure," I said.

Just west of Rio Vista the land changed suddenly from flat to low rolling hills. It was as though the Sacramento River had blocked the hills and wouldn't let them get across to wrinkle up the flat land. The road swung in curves through the hills and rose and fell, tracing the flow of the land. Strong wind blew in the canyon that the road followed, and on the hills amber-colored grass moved in the wind, changing color to gold or tan when the wind gusts changed direction.

Low farm buildings and the shortest windmills I'd ever seen were built in arroyos. Sycamore and eucalyptus trees grew in the arroyos around the buildings. Sheep grazed on the grass.

"It's always windy through here," Gene said.

I didn't say anything. I was imagining the hills as breasts. Giant breasts. The hills looked exactly like women's breasts to me; well, they looked exactly how I thought women's breasts looked. Hills on both sides of the road mounding up like huge breasts, coming together like the deep cleft between breasts, the pickup traveling along in the cleavage of breasts, Gene Tole driving, me riding shotgun, rolling hills everywhere, as far as I could see, hills like thighs, hills like ass cheeks and legs, hills that came together like the place where a woman's legs come together, pickup riding along the road up the thigh through a grove of scrub oak trees growing right where you'd expect them to be growing.

I had to scoot my butt around on the pickup seat to get comfortable, pull my pant legs down, rearrange things. My new Levi's weren't the only thing stiff now, and I didn't want to embarrass myself any more than I already had. I looked over at Gene to see if he had noticed the bulge in my pants, but he was intent on looking out his window.

"Coast live oak," he said, pointing at the trees, "*Quercus agrifolia*." He looked at me and grinned.

"Got it?" he said.

"Sure do," I said.

Mariposa Means Butterfly, Means More

 "WELL, THERE IT IS," GENE SAID, "Luther Burbank's garden."

"That's it?" I said.

Gene pulled up in front of an ordinary house on an ordinary street and shut the pickup engine off. Everything I could see in every direction was ordinary. In the parking strip there was a black metal sign with gold painted letters: HOME OF LUTHER BURBANK, it said. Gene Tole wasn't kidding me.

The house looked like the kind of house a five-year-old kid would draw with crayons, front windows the eyes, front door the mouth. Climbing roses grew on a white picket fence along the front that enclosed the house and garden and separated them from the street.

Gene and I let ourselves in through a gate in the picket fence. The garden was quiet and I closed the gate carefully so as not to make any noise. I stood there for a moment to take it in. Luther Burbank's house was old and plain, like it had been shipped directly from New England. The house looked clean, freshly painted—white with dark green around the windows. Lace curtains hung in the upstairs window. Everything in the garden was tidy, not a leaf out of place.

Gene walked ahead, peering around to see if anyone was there. I felt as if Gene and I were sneaking into the garden, like we didn't really belong there. Gene left the brick walkway that went to the front door and followed a pea-gravel path around the side of the house to the back porch. Every step we took, the pea gravel crunched so loud you could hear it a block away.

An old Mexican man in bib overalls came from behind a two-story building that looked like it had been shipped from New England, too. The old man wheeled a wheelbarrow in front of him. He set the wheelbarrow down, removed his battered felt hat, and wiped his forehead on the sleeve of his blue work shirt.

He said, "No hablo Ingles," and pointed toward the back of the house.

The door opened and a young man with brown hair and a thick mustache came out on the back porch.

"Chris. How the hell are you?" Gene said.

The young man jumped right off the back porch, not

bothering to take the steps, and landed on the wide gravel space in front of Gene.

Chris grabbed Gene Tole around the shoulders and hugged him. Gene hugged back, one arm over Chris's shoulder, the other arm wrapped around Chris's back.

Chris was calling Gene a "bloke" and saying "excellent" a whole bunch of times. Then Chris rested his head on Gene's shoulder.

"God, it's good to see you," Chris said.

Must be how people in England greet each other, I thought. I mean, what else could explain it? Never before had I seen two men hug each other. Not in real life. Not in the movies. Not anywhere. I had never seen my father hug his brother, Martin, like that. I had never seen my father hug my mother like that, not even when my father and mother were still happy together.

I stepped back a bit and pushed my fists hard into the pockets of my new Levi's. I rocked back and forth on my heels and toes and looked at the cream-colored rubber tips of my new Keds. Gene was my friend, we rode all the way to Santa Rosa together in the pickup, we were building the garden together, and I didn't much care for Chris Rudd and his English ways. I looked at the building; on top of the roof was a birdhouselike structure with shutters on the sides and a weather vane on top.

"This is Christopher Rudd," Gene said to me.

Gene put his hand on my shoulder for a moment to pull

me into the company of his friend from England. I shook Christopher Rudd's hand. My throat was dry. I didn't say anything—wasn't sure my voice would come out right.

"This is Dave Ryan," Gene said.

"Ah," Chris said, "so this is your protégé."

I said *protégé* over and over in my head to remember it. Made a note to look up *protégé* in the dictionary when I got home.

"Come into the kitchen. I'll make some tea," Chris said. "Mrs. Burbank lives in the house—upstairs mostly—but she's away for a couple weeks. We share the kitchen."

"Where are your digs?" Gene said.

"In the carriage house," Chris said. He pointed to the large windows on the second story of the carriage house; there was a stairway that went up the side of the building to a landing and door.

Chris put his arm over Gene's shoulder, and they walked toward the house side by side like that. Gene turned around, waving his arm for me to come in, too, for a cup of tea.

Chris put a kettle of water on the stove to boil.

"Have yourself a look around," Chris said to me, and he and Gene talked of people and things I didn't know about.

I walked slowly into the front rooms of Luther Burbank's house. Even though Mrs. Burbank still lived upstairs, the other rooms of the house were kept like a museum; it was as if Luther Burbank's house had been frozen, as if he'd just stepped out to mail a letter and would be back in a minute. But the plaque by the front door said Luther Burbank died in 1926, thirty-one years ago, and it seemed to me about time someone moved the furniture around, freshened things up a bit.

Books filled shelves in the living room. Books written by Luther Burbank about plant breeding sat on a desk. Beside the books on the desk was a framed picture of three men standing together. Typed on a card beneath the picture it said: *Luther Burbank, Thomas Edison, and Henry Ford together in San Francisco to address an audience at the 1914 World's Fair, "The Panama Exposition."* The three men were dressed up, all dapper, Mr. Burbank resting both hands on a cane propped in front of him.

"Gardener's knees," Gene said later when I showed him the picture.

If I hadn't gotten bored then, gotten tired of looking at Mr. Burbank's dusty stuff, if I hadn't told Chris Rudd I didn't care for tea, tea in my mind being for old ladies and the English, I may never have learned about *mariposa*, even though I didn't understand at the time, didn't understand because Pete, the old Mexican laborer, couldn't speak English and I didn't know Spanish, or because I just wasn't ready to understand.

It was Pete, speaking Spanish, who told me of *mariposa*, *mariposa* being the Spanish word for butterfly—meaning butterfly, meaning more.

I left the house and was wandering around the gravel path at Luther Burbank's garden by myself, reading painted metal signs about plants Mr. Burbank had hybridized. That's how I met Pete, who wore bib overalls and a battered felt hat. He was short and stocky, and patches of white whiskers showed on his weathered face.

"Pete," he said, pointing to his chest. "Pete Corales. ¿Sí?" I nodded. Said "Sí," which about did in my Spanish.

I said "Dave," and pointed to my chest, too. That's how Pete and I understood each other. We understood that if we wanted to talk, we had to talk without speaking, had to talk with our hands, by shrugging our shoulders, grinning and nodding.

Pete motioned with his hand for me to follow him. He acted as though he had a treasure in the garden he wanted to show off, some gift he would share with me that was not for just anyone to see.

It was odd. Even though we'd just met, even though we couldn't speak the same language, even though Pete looked to be at least seventy and I was fourteen, it felt as if we were longtime friends. Pete and I may as well have both been seventy, both been thirteen, both speaking Spanish, or both English. Maybe we both felt lonely, or like we didn't quite fit in. Maybe Pete thought I was feeling lost; maybe he needed someone to talk to, or a way to feel important. Anyway, we ignored the differences and acted on what was the same. Pete showed me around the garden, shared its secrets, its magic.

I followed Pete to the carriage house. Next to the carriage house door was a bronze faucet that stood about two feet high on a galvanized pipe. A stone that had been hollowed out by Indians to make a bowl for grinding acorns was placed on smooth river rocks under the faucet to catch water. Reeds and shamrock grew up through the river rocks around the bowl, and moss grew in the cracks between them.

Pete turned on the faucet and fanned his hand through the water until he felt it was cold. Water splashed into the bowl and spilled over onto the rocks. The rocks were shiny and the moss was dark green. Pete put his hand out, offering me the first drink. I bent down and cupped my hands to catch water from the faucet and brought the water to my mouth again and again to drink. I stepped back and straightened up and dried my lips and chin on the sleeve of my new shirt. Pete bent down and cupped water in his hands and drank, too.

Pete took his felt hat off and splashed water on his face and over his white hair; he held his head under the faucet and moved his head back and forth in a slow swinging motion. He stepped back and shook his head. He stood up and pulled the shirttail from inside his bib overalls and dried his face and hair. He took a red bandanna from his back pocket and tied it around his head, knot in back. Then he put his felt hat back on. He looked at me a moment, paused, then grinned and raised his right index finger in the air beside his head.

I looked around. The sun was directly overhead. The garden was filled with bright light, the air still, leaves hushed on trees. Pete relaxed his finger and lowered his hand, slowly reaching out toward me. He took hold of my shirt just above the pocket and pulled me toward him. He was backing up, still holding me by the shirt.

Pete let go of my shirt and turned around. He walked toward a small wooden toolshed built like the carriage house.

What happened next was not a sci-fi sort of thing you'd see in the movies—no spaceship landed, no giant insects escaped a scientist's lab—but it was spooky and weird enough for me.

Pete turned his head to make sure I was behind him. I followed along the path past the toolshed and turned toward the back of the garden. Overhead the sky was a great white dome, the garden without shadow.

When we rounded the corner of the toolshed, a rich deep sound, barely audible and eerie, moved in the air. The skin on the back of my neck felt crawly; I rubbed my neck with both hands and ran my hands through my hair a bunch of times to scratch my head. A deep vibrating hum was in the air. It was a presence. Then the first butterfly lit on the gravel path in front of me. Above me three butterflies flew in ragged patterns against the white sky. Beside the path a huge old apple tree grew flat against a heavy trellis. The tree leaves were dense and blocked the view beyond. Hundreds of butterflies lit on top of the apple tree, and some fluttered crazily down the side of the tree next to me. They acted like they were drunk.

Pete went behind the trellis and I couldn't see him anymore, couldn't hear his steps on the gravel path. At the end of the trellis I turned and entered a small open area—an out-door room—and there thousands and thousands of butter-flies covered everything. Butterflies flew in jerky, zigzag movements through the air. Large, bright, yellow and blue-black butterflies, wings looking wet, flopping, bumping into one another, fighting for a place to be in the world. Against the back fence a large shrub was covered with butterflies, butterflies so thick I couldn't see the leaves, couldn't see the long purple flowers at first. The butterflies spilled off the shrub and covered the gravel around it, covered the fence behind it; they covered the raised flower beds near the shrub. Butterflies that were perched moved their wings slowly, flashed iridescent blue, drying their wings in the sunshine, sucking sweetness from the flowers, warmth from the sun and air.

Pete stood in the center of the open space. He held his felt hat in his hand, both arms lifted into the air to greet the butterflies, to embrace them. I moved carefully into the out-door room and stood beside him. Pete and I stood silently watching the butterflies like that for a long time. Pete put his hat back on his head and dropped his arms.

I could pet them if I wanted, I thought.

"*Mariposa*," Pete whispered.

"What?" I said.

"*Mariposa*," he said. He touched a butterfly with the tip of his finger.

"*Sí*," I said. He was giving them a name.

Pete held out his hand to the butterflies; five or six butterflies landed on his arm. He was intent, motionless.

Then Pete moved closer to the shrub, placing his feet carefully so as not to step on the insects on the ground. Butterflies landed on Pete's hat and on his shoulders. I moved closer to the shrub, too. Butterflies came toward me and I felt them land on my hair and on my shoulders and I watched them covering my outstretched arms. I felt butterfly feet, rough and wiry on my hands, grasping my skin, holding on to my skin with a light pinch. I felt a butterfly land on my ear, feet clutching, wings jerking, and another land on my forehead, sticking to my eyebrow and skin. Pinching there. Wing flapping, bumping, hitting my eyelash, my cheek.

It was too much. I waved my arms wildly and jumped away from the shrub, brushing at my face with my hands, crushing butterflies on the gravel under my feet.

Pete came up next to me. He stood looking over his shoulder at Luther Burbank's house beyond the toolshed, mostly hidden in the trees and shrubs. He pointed, secretively, wanting me to look at the house, too, his head close to mine like we were conspirators. It made me feel sneaky, as if I was spying, seeing what shouldn't be seen. I looked toward the house where he pointed anyway. I couldn't see the kitchen window, Gene or Chris, but they were there. They were in the house. Pete put his face close to my face; his felt hat bumped against my head.

"*Mariposa*," he said, still pointing.

He whispered, "*Mariposa*."

"*Sí*," I said, but I didn't understand.

I thought Pete wanted me to tell Gene and Chris about the butterflies drying their wings on the shrub. I nodded yes to Pete, because I thought I knew what he meant, but I didn't know. I didn't know what he was telling me at all.

"*Mariposa*," Pete said. He put the back of his wrist on his hip, his other hand he held high in the air and he turned around, his feet prancing, flipping his hands and wrists.

"*Mariposa*," he said. He threw his head back and laughed hard and loud, bent over forward now, slapping his hands on his knees, head back again, laughing a hard silent laugh and then letting out a high shriek.

Inside his mouth was dark, his teeth stained brown; many teeth were missing, the rest worn down to the gum.

Pete lifted his hat and fanned his face with it. The red bandanna on his head made him look like a gypsy. I ran to the house to get Gene and Chris to tell them about the butterflies, so they could see them, too.

Inside the kitchen I didn't even wait for Gene and Chris to leave a space in their talk for me to say something; I just butted right in.

"There's a shrub out there completely covered with butterflies," I said. "Butterflies everywhere, just hatching. You can hold them in your hand, they land all over you."

"The shrub have gray foliage? Dark blue flowers, sort of like lilacs?" Gene asked.

"Yeah," I said. "Only you can't even see the shrub, it's all covered with butterflies."

"It's a butterfly bush," Gene said. "*Buddleia alternifolia*."

He stood up. "Think we ought to plant one of those for you and your mother?"

"Sure," I said. But I wasn't really so hot on the idea of having our garden be under attack from a swarm of wet-winged insects every time they decided to hatch.

Gene, Chris, and I went outside to get a look at the butterflies. Pete was gone.

Later in the afternoon, when Gene and I were ready to leave, I went around the garden to find Pete. I didn't see him anywhere. It was time to go. Gene said we needed to get started, and so I left Luther Burbank's garden without seeing Pete again or saying good-bye to him. Didn't get to use my other Spanish word, didn't say, "Adios."

Pizza Pie and City Lights

"HOW'S IT SOUND TO GO HOME through San Francisco?" Gene asked.

"Sounds great," I said.

Gene turned the pickup south on Highway 101, and we drove through Petaluma, through San Rafael and Sausalito. At Sausalito the highway climbed high over a hill with houses and gardens stacked up on it. Every once in a while I glimpsed San Francisco Bay over the housetops, through the trees. When we got to the crest of the hill, I thought of the roller coaster at Santa Cruz—that's how steep it was going down the other side toward the water of San Francisco Bay. As if that weren't enough, right there in front of us stood the towers of the Golden Gate Bridge poking into the sky.

There we were, Gene Tole and I, scooting down that

grade in the Studebaker, shooting lickety-split onto the Golden Gate Bridge, about like flying, my heart soaring, could hardly get my breath my stomach pushing into my chest so much.

Gene drove the pickup along the outside lane of the Golden Gate Bridge and I could see the mountains of Marin County where they came right down to the ocean, waves breaking against the rocky mountain edges.

Outside the window where I had my arm propped, a huge band of cables rose up to the tip of the bridge tower. Gene and I were rolling along on the Golden Gate Bridge, passing through the tower, the cable high overhead, descending now in a slow curve. Sunlight shone between smaller cables that dropped to hold the span and made shadows like a picket fence on the bridge surface. All together it made me dizzy.

On the far end of the bridge we came to the hills of the Presidio, covered with trees; a thick wall of fog rolled over the hills, pushing its way toward downtown San Francisco.

The sun burned bright on the hills of San Francisco, on the houses, and on the skyscrapers downtown. The sun was like a spotlight focused on the city; details stood out, looking more real than real. San Francisco looked exotic, like a foreign city you'd see in a *National Geographic*—Sorrento maybe, or Capri.

Gene took a ramp off the bridge and we circled through the Presidio and onto a city street. The houses along the street were so close together, the walls butted up against each other. Many of the houses had garage doors under them and steep narrow steps leading to the front door. Some of the houses were painted bright colors, and had stained shingle siding with dark-colored trim; other houses, made of stucco, were painted vivid pastel colors.

"There's the Palace of Fine Arts, the one that looks like a Roman ruin." Gene pointed to the left. "It's the only building left from the Panama-Pacific Exposition of 1915."

The building made me think of the picture of Luther Burbank, Henry Ford, and Thomas Edison I'd seen on Mr. Burbank's desk. At the tops of columns stood statues of nude women resting their arms on the dome roof they supported. The nude women looked tired and worn out. Couldn't blame them for being tired if they'd been holding up the roof like that since 1915. We cruised along Lombard Street, headed into the main part of the city. We zigzagged over a few streets and went through a long tunnel and came out on Broadway.

"That's Coit Tower on top of that hill in front of us," Gene said. "We're in North Beach now."

There was no beach anywhere, but I decided not to mention it. We weren't on a main road anymore; we were in the heart of a neighborhood. The sidewalks were packed with people. Cafés along the street didn't have walls, had windows instead that opened from floor to ceiling, and people sat inside and out just like it was the same. Don't they have flies in San Francisco? I wondered. Decided not to mention that either.

"Now, the trick is to find a parking place," Gene said. "Then we call your ma."

Gene found a parking place and pulled in. When I got out of the pickup, I jumped up and down a few times right there on the sidewalk I was so excited. I stretched my arms out and swung them back and forth a bit, too. I couldn't wait to look around. The sky was clear. A strong wind blew from the west, made my shirt ruffle, Gene's vest flap.

Gene put money in the parking meter and pointed out a pay phone in front of a drugstore across the street. We crossed the street to a plaza. There were wide low steps at the back of the plaza that went up to the doors of a church.

"You want to talk to your ma?"

"No, you go ahead."

"Why don't you stay here, then, while I call her."

Gene walked three doors down the street to the drugstore. I sat on a bench in the plaza. I kept my eye on Gene leaning up against the drugstore wall, his head hidden under the awning, while I waited for him to get off the phone.

The plaza was paved with brick, and three California pepper trees grew along the street. A statue of Christopher Columbus was in the center of the plaza. Old men wearing black suits sat together playing checkers, and all over the plaza pigeons strutted around cooing, pecking the pavement and one another. I felt warm, inside and out, sitting in the late-afternoon sun waiting for Gene. I was watching the sun on the pigeons' feathers, the sun making the feathers shine the colors of oil on water.

"We're all set," Gene said. "She's happy we're having a good time. How about something to eat? I'm starved," he said. "This is an Italian neighborhood. Let's get some spaghetti. Or how about a pizza pie, maybe?"

"What's pizza pie?" I said.

"Never had it?" Gene said. "It's great. You'll love it."

"Okay," I said. "I'm starved, too."

We walked toward the hill that Coit Tower stood on and looked up a street so narrow it could have passed for an alley. At the end of the street was a two-story building with a storefront on the ground floor. A sign saying MARIO'S hung over the door. It looked like people lived upstairs—curtains on the windows, flowerpots on the sills. Just before we got to Mario's, the door under the sign swung open and three women and two men came out speaking Italian, their arms, hands, and faces speaking Italian, too. They were either really happy or really mad; whichever, they were enjoying themselves.

That wasn't so remarkable, though. What was remarkable was the blast of garlic smell that escaped out the door of Mario's with them. Garlic smell and the sound of people singing opera.

"God almighty," Gene said. "This is the place. What do you think?" All the time Gene was saying this, he was walking faster toward Mario's.

"Looks good, sounds fine, smells great," I said. What the heck, I figured, what do I know? Gene stood holding the door open. The garlic smell was thick.

My first thought when we got inside was that we had made a mistake: it looked like we were in somebody's house, it looked like a family reunion was going on. Two old couples, grandparents I figured, sat at one end of a plank table. They were dressed in black, or blue so dark it may as well have been black; their arms rested on red-and-white-checkered oilcloth. Two other plank tables covered with oilcloth were filled with aunt and uncle folk. Kids ran around everywhere.

At the far end of the room was a counter with red, white, and green Christmas tree lights strung around it. Behind the counter a man and woman worked in a kitchen cooking. Must be Mario, I thought, and Mrs. Mario. A large black oven covered a side wall in the kitchen.

Gene and I sat down at the end of the long table with the two old Italian couples at the other end. They were eating spaghetti and drinking red wine. The women wore white lace shawls over their shoulders.

A girl about high-school age came to our end of the table—the daughter, Miss Mario, I figured. Gene ordered.

"We'd like a large pizza pie with everything on it," he said.

"Anchovies?"

"Everything except anchovies. You don't want anchovies, do you, Ace?" Gene looked at me.

"What are anchovies?"

"Salty little fish."

"Don't sound like something I'd want," I said.

"Fine," Gene said. "No anchovies, and I'd like a glass of

Chianti. What do you want to drink?" he said to me. "Other than Chianti, that is." Gene grinned wide as if he was the cleverest guy in San Francisco. I thought he just might be.

Miss Mario brought this glorious-looking full-moon pizza pie to the end of the table where Gene and I sat. Gene lifted a piece of pizza from the round full moon with one hand, slid the fingers of his other hand under it, and scooped the slice to a plate Miss Mario had brought over along with a pile of napkins. Just how messy does she expect us to be? I wondered when she brought over that pile of napkins. Now I understood.

I pulled a piece of pizza away from the pie. My slice didn't want to let go of the rest of the pizza pie. I pulled long strings of white and yellow cheese with my finger, winding the cheese strings around my finger like Gene did, and scraped the cheese back on my slice of pizza.

This was the only problem I had with eating pizza. When I took a big first bite, I wolfed pizza into my mouth like I knew exactly how to eat it, but the bite of pizza pie bit me right back. The cheese and sauce were so hot, they stuck to the roof of my mouth, front to back, and burned there before I could pry them off with my tongue. I practically swallowed that bite of pizza whole after juggling it around my mouth with my tongue, guzzling water over the bite of pizza to cool it down. Thank God for the water Miss Mario had brought to the table.

"You all right?" Gene said.

"Fine." I nodded my head. "Just fine."

Tears tried to get over my eyelids and tell Gene I was lying. Tears telling everyone in Mario's I was lying, telling everyone in Mario's I didn't know the first thing about how to eat pizza, didn't know beans about Italian food, neighbor of the Pasacco girls or not.

But I loved pizza. I was sorry I couldn't taste it better after burning myself on the first bite like that; the skin on the roof of my mouth was loose and flapping every time I took a bite, and my tongue was not doing such a great job tasting the pizza either. But I could taste enough to know I loved pizza and wanted to have it again. Pizza was just about the best food I'd ever had. I mean, hamburgers were still big, maybe they were the best, but pizza was right up there.

Gene and I sat at the table for a while after we finished eating. Gene rested his elbows on the red-and-white-checkered oilcloth. I did the same. It wasn't like Gene and I were part of the family reunion feeling at Mario's, people who knew one another coming and going, but I felt warm sitting there and watching, listening to the sad songs of opera, not able to understand, but understanding.

Gene played with the wax dripping from the candle in the wine bottle on the table between us, wax all different colors dripping on the straw stuff around the bulge in the bottle. Gene made a little dent in the lip of the candle with his finger. The wax drained away from the flame and made a bright splotch of purple wax on the straw stuff.

Miss Mario came by with a bottle of wine just like the one holding the candle.

"More Chianti?" She smiled at Gene and waited for his answer like she was hanging from a cliff and couldn't get her next breath until she found out if Gene wanted more Chianti.

"Sure. It's nice," Gene said.

Miss Mario leaned way forward over the table and filled Gene's glass with Chianti.

"Thank you," Gene said.

Miss Mario smiled, her eyes looked down, pretending to be modest, but she had her hand on her waist, her hip pushed forward.

"My treat," she said.

"Well, thank you," Gene said again.

Gene looked across the table at me. He winked. Miss Mario left our table and went back to the counter. She kept glancing back at Gene every chance she had. Gene sipped Chianti from his wineglass. Miss Mario couldn't get enough of looking at him. I began to wonder if we were going to have three people riding back to Stockton in the old pickup cab.

"Dinner's on me." Gene stood up and reached into his back pocket for his wallet.

"I can get mine." I fumbled around trying to get my money out of the watch pocket of my Levi's.

"Forget it." Gene put his hand on my shoulder. "It's on me."

The way he said "It's on me," I didn't argue anymore. I

went to the doorway of Mario's and stood on the steps looking out at the narrow street. The sun had gone down and the wind quit blowing. The sky was dark blue now; soon it would be dark. I looked back into the warm light, candles flickering in bottles dripping wax, and Miss Mario watching Gene as he walked away from her toward the door, and I saw that she started to say something to Gene as he passed, reached her hand out slightly toward him, but didn't say anything. Maybe she wanted to ask him to stay longer, to stay so she could get to know him better, so they could be friends. I wondered how Miss Mario had known so quickly that Gene Tole was a special man.

Gene and I walked down the street, both smelling like garlic.

"Is there any place in Stockton that makes pizza?" I asked. Gene and I were headed back toward Broadway, where we had parked the pickup.

"Just the Gay Nineties on El Dorado Street," he said. "The only place I know of in Stockton that makes pizza, right there across El Dorado Street from Eden Square. It's kind of a tavern, but young people, people your age, go there for pizza. The bartenders and waiters wear gay nineties clothes—straw hats, garters on their arms to hold up their sleeves. You know what I'm talking about?"

"Sure," I said, but I didn't, exactly.

"There's a balcony upstairs and you can sit up there and eat pizza, have a Coke, and watch folks downstairs at the bar."

"Bar?" I said.

"I think you'd like the pizza," Gene said. "There's a back room, too, but you wouldn't want to go in there. It's like a private club. Don't go in there, but the balcony is fine."

Gene stretched his arms above his head and laced his fingers together, palms turned out. Then he swung his arms back and forth like he was a big-league pitcher warming up.

"I could go for a nice cup of coffee before we get back on the road," Gene said. "You want something? What do you say?"

"I'll pass," I said, "unless maybe we see a place with ice cream."

I was thinking of cooling my mouth down after the pizza, cooling it where the pizza had bitten the roof of my mouth. Gene and I strolled along Broadway for a block, looking in windows, keeping an eye out for a coffee and ice cream place. The sidewalk along Broadway was crowded with young people who dressed like they didn't have any money and didn't care how they looked.

"Beatniks," Gene said. "Read about them in the newspaper." He nodded at several groups of people we passed.

That's where we were, looking for coffee and ice cream along Broadway, watching beatniks, when we found the City Lights Bookstore, the door propped open. Bright light from bare bulbs on the ceiling shone out to the sidewalk and drew us in.

"This is great," Gene said. "Let's have a look." He was already through the doorway when he said it.

The City Lights Bookstore was crowded and hot. Just about every person in the City Lights was wearing black or dirty denim. People kept bumping into one another; even when I was hardly moving I bumped into people. I stood still trying to see everything without looking like I was trying to see everything. I bumped into a woman with straight brown hair cut in an upside-down bowl style.

"Excuse me," I said.

"That's cool," the woman said, and gave me a big smile.

I wondered if her big smile was because she liked me or because I looked funny, my madras shirt glowing like a neon sign among all the black clothes. My madras shirt flashing "hick," flashing "fresh off the farm, folks" to the beatniks in the City Lights Bookstore.

I stepped back from the woman. She was a bona fide beatnik. She wore a skintight black thing over all of her body and a short leather skirt that covered her middle. You could see right through the black thing. I tried hard not to look. Looked anyway. Her breasts moved under the black thing. It was easy to see her nipples.

When I managed to turn away, I bumped into three people at once. Bumped into a man who wore a white T-shirt with a black leather vest and blue jeans, sandals on his feet, practically barefoot in a crowd like this. He took a long draw on a cigarette, tilted his head back, and blew smoke at the ceiling. He ignored me, moved away like I wasn't there, like we hadn't bumped.

The City Lights Bookstore was electric. It was like someone had plugged the place into a huge socket and electric current charged through the air, bouncing off the walls, the ceiling, and floor. Bouncing off the people, too, the people bouncing off one another.

This place would have books that would tell me a lot more about what I wanted to know than *Madame Bovary* did. I moved around, pressing between people. Gene was looking at tables of books. I browsed the shelves, edged slowly along reading titles and pulling books out to see the pictures on the covers and read what it said about the book on the back. Most of the books were paperback, but a different-type paperback book than was at the drug or grocery stores in Stockton.

The City Lights had different rooms and I followed the wall around a corner and went through a wide arch into the next room. A sign by the arch said HUMAN LANDSCAPES in raised black letters. The walls were white and hung with black-and-white photographs held behind glass with metal clips at the corners.

This room was packed with people, too. I thought of Gene telling me about the Gay Nineties in Stockton and about the back room there. "Don't go in the back room," he'd said. I wondered if this was what Gene meant by a back room, if the back room at the Gay Nineties was like this. I eased through people on my way toward a wall so I could see the photographs.

I hate to admit how slow I was in catching on to these pictures. I looked at all the pictures on one wall. They looked like landscapes, looked familiar. But they weren't landscapes, weren't familiar. I moved along to the next wall. The first photograph on this wall reminded me of the hills Gene and I drove through this morning, the hills west of Rio Vista. I looked closely at it again. That's when I figured it out.

The picture was of the bottom of a foot. The camera was focused on the underside of a big toe and the toe next to it and the ball of a foot. I could make out the lines on the flesh, which were like thumbprints, felt proud of myself figuring it out.

I went back to the photograph I just passed on the other wall. The first time I looked at the picture I thought it might be of a mesa, like in New Mexico or Arizona. It looked like rough rocky earth around the base, cliffs rising straight up, flat on top. But what it was, I could see it clearly now, was a woman's nipple popped up, filling almost all the picture, filling the picture so a person couldn't make it out at first.

I went back to see another picture. What I'd thought was maybe reeds on a riverbank the first time, I saw was actually hair on a woman's private part. I mean, I think that's what it was. I couldn't be sure. I studied it carefully, but I wasn't sure.

What made me think the photograph was of a woman's private part was when I figured out the photograph next to it. The picture next to it looked like a bare hill filling almost the entire glass. But this was no hill. This was the end of a man's penis, the end of a man's penis all hard and smooth. I couldn't believe it. Some guy getting his penis hard and then letting some other guy—I figured it must be a guy—take a picture of the hard penis that way.

It was much too warm in the back room for me, bumping into people, body to body. I didn't feel comfortable rubbing against people anymore, not in the condition I was in. I didn't want Gene to find me with my nose pressed against pictures of people's body parts, nothing between my nose and body parts but a piece of clear glass.

Gene was still in the room with windows onto the street when I walked back through the arch. I looked around in there some more, too, hoping to cool down, start breathing again. I found a book called *Maggie Cassidy* by Jack Kerouac. This is what it said on the back of the book: "A story of the pain, embarrassment and intense joy of first love. Kerouac's novel is a moving, nostalgic and semiautobiographical picture of a New England adolescent."

There was a picture of Jack Kerouac on the back, too, and that's what I liked most. That's what sold me on the book, the picture of Jack Kerouac. He was the handsomest man I had ever seen, large sad eyes that told a story themselves and lips rounded and perfect.

"Ready to go?" Gene said. He stood beside me but didn't ask to see the book I was holding.

Gene had a paper bag from the City Lights Bookstore wedged under his arm. I wondered what he bought, but didn't ask.

"Sure," I said. "I want to get this first, though."

I took *Maggie Cassidy* to the counter, hoped my face

wasn't red. Behind the cash register was a tall man dressed in a white robe that looked like something the Pope would wear. He wore a round skull cap that matched the Pope's robe he wore.

"That be all for you?" he said.

"Yes, thank you." I put my forefinger and thumb into the watch pocket of my new Levi's and took out the folded ten-dollar bill that I had intended to bring back to my mother. It took a moment to get the bill unfolded. I smoothed it out and handed it to the man.

Gene and I walked out of the City Lights Bookstore and started back along Broadway to where we parked the pickup.

"The guy at the counter was Ferlinghetti," Gene said.

"Ferlin who?" I said.

"Lawrence Ferlinghetti," Gene said. "I've seen his picture in the paper. He's one of the Beat poets."

"Oh," I said, and wondered if I had treated the man behind the cash register, dressed like the Pope, with enough respect. But all he had said was, "That be all for you?" and that didn't sound so poetic to me. How was I to know? He took my ten-dollar bill all right and gave me some change. He couldn't have been too offended.

Home
After
Dark

 "GOD! SMELL THAT COFFEE ROAST-
ing," Gene said. He rolled his window down all the way and
turned his nose toward the opening, took some deep breaths.
Almost nine-thirty and the evening smelled like breakfast to
me. The pickup climbed a ramp that rose in a slow graceful
curve up through an old industrial section of San Francisco.

"South of Mission," Gene said.

We were heading toward the first tower of the San Francisco Bay Bridge. The ramp passed by the upper floors of factory buildings. Through the lighted windows of a factory I
saw a man without a shirt on loading cloth sacks onto a hand
truck. Attached to the side of the brick building was the
huge lighted figure of a man dressed like one of the three
wise men, full yellow robe to his bare feet, turban on his

head, and holding a bowl in his hands raised before him like he was making an offering. Large red letters below the man said, FOLGERS. I recognized him from the side of coffee cans. We passed just above his knees, a ripple painted in his yellow robe to look like he was moving.

I felt like the Studebaker was airborne; the concrete band we traveled soared above the buildings of the Mission District, no landmarks remained to ground us. High above on the Bay Bridge towers, a blue light flashed a warning to airplanes. Over my shoulder, out the rear window, the lights of San Francisco glittered, stacked up on hills and on one another, prettier than any picture I had ever seen and more exciting.

"Yerba Buena Island," Gene said. The pickup entered a tunnel on the side of a mountain in the bay. Inside the tunnel was white tile and bright lights. Streams of traffic flowed in both directions, all these people coming from and going to San Francisco, I thought; it made me feel small.

Outside the tunnel the bridge soared again over the bay and ahead of us I saw the edge of San Francisco Bay—drawn clearly by lights, dense until they were stopped by the water.

"Over there to the left is Berkeley," Gene said. "Oakland is directly ahead of us and Alameda to the right." He pointed, his finger almost touching the windshield.

In front of us was a faint horizon of dark blue hills, behind the hills the night sky was a dense blue-black; it was rich and deep and went on forever. No stars shone yet in the sky, no moon. Lights from houses and streets shone thick and bright all over the hills and onto the flatland the bridge ramps dropped down to. I thought about the people who lived behind the lights in houses on the hills and on the flatland, and I thought of the stories of their lives and how important the people were to themselves and how I knew nothing about them or what was going on in their lives and that I didn't really care because I didn't know them, but that I did care because they were people just like me and even if I didn't know them personally they were important, just like they didn't know me and I was important. I was feeling really small. Insignificant.

Gene gave the man at the gate some money for letting us cross the bridge and we got on the Nimitz Freeway, which took us over part of Oakland. We left Oakland and were headed toward the Altamont Pass, toward the Livermore Valley and home, when Gene started to talk. Gene spoke quietly, as if he were alone, as if talking to himself, but he was talking to me. I liked listening to Gene talk, his voice deep and soft. His words came out in an easy rhythm. He started with a simple question.

"What are you thinking about?" he asked.

"Not much," I said. "Just thinking about all those people behind those lights on the hills and thinking about what their lives are like."

"That sounds like a lot of thinking to me," Gene said. It was quiet in the pickup for a moment. "What do you suppose their lives are like?" he said. "Do you suppose they're all families sitting around eating dinner together? Mom, Dad, and the kids?"

"No," I said. "I suppose there're all kinds of people behind those lights, not all families sitting around, but single people, married people, and widowed."

"Separated and divorced, too?"

"Yeah, that too."

"I can't imagine what it would be like to have my mother and father split up."

"It's not so great, I'll tell you that much. I don't recommend it."

Gene chuckled, looked over at me.

"You don't, huh. What caused your mom and dad to separate, you think?"

"I don't know exactly." I wasn't holding back; I didn't know. "I was there, but I didn't know what was going on. May as well have been somewhere else."

"That can happen."

We were quiet again for a while.

Gene relaxed back in the pickup seat, driving with one hand, resting his other arm on the window edge. We passed through the hills that separate Oakland and the East Bay from Castro Valley. The pickup rolled across the flat floor of Castro Valley.

"You miss your dad much?" Gene said.

"I miss him," I said.

Then a feeling of being dishonest came over me; I felt

bad, like I wasn't telling Gene the truth, wasn't telling him how I really felt about Dad, not telling all of it.

My throat got tight. I swallowed a bunch of times to make the tightness go away, but it didn't. Sometimes I didn't miss Dad at all—that was the truth—sometimes I didn't even think about him. Sometimes I was glad I didn't have to see Dad anymore, but I didn't say any of that to Gene.

It wasn't just that I didn't tell Gene all the truth about Dad that made me feel awful; mostly, what made me feel awful was that I didn't love my father. I didn't love Dad like other kids loved their dads—like I knew I was supposed to love mine.

"What's he like? Your dad?"

"I don't know. I don't know what he's like. He's like most other men, I guess. Why do you ask?"

"I was just thinking how it must be for you being separated from your dad—your brother, too. My mother and father were together until my mother died. I don't have your experience."

"I didn't think I'd miss my brother," I said. "I thought I hated him. We used to fight all the time. But now I miss him. I like him now. He was sick a lot with asthma when we were young. Brad got all the attention; he was loved and worried over—I was just there. That's how it felt to me—I know that it wasn't so, but that's how it felt. I miss Brad now. I think about him and wonder what he's doing, if he's all right."

"It's not that way with your dad, though, huh?" Gene said. "You don't wonder what he's doing, if he's all right?"

"I don't know Dad. I lived all my life with Dad, until now, but I don't know him. He's not very friendly."

"Not friendly?"

"Not to his family. Dad's friendly enough to other people—the neighbors, or strangers—but not to us, not to Ma or Brad or to me."

"Seems odd, doesn't it?" Gene looked over at me, green light from the dashboard lighting his face.

"Yeah. It is odd. It was like he didn't like us much, didn't want to be around us. It was like everyone else was more important to him than we were."

Gene double-clutched, shifting down, his fist resting over the gearshift knob that came up from the floor between us. I looked out the window; Gene and I had left the flat floor of Castro Valley and were climbing a range of hills. The Studebaker pulled hard on the grade and we weren't going fast anymore.

"Think your ma got tired of that? Of being unimportant. Think that's what made her leave?"

"No. It was more than that. Ma was used to that. I think what did it was that one night when they fought he hit her. Dad hit Ma and it was never okay again after that." After the words were out, I couldn't believe I'd said them.

"Jesus, I guess not."

Then, without intending to, I told Gene the story of my

mother and father's separation, the story I didn't know I knew until I started telling it.

We were riding along in the Studebaker pickup, going over the Altamont Pass, Gene listening, once in a while throwing in a question, a comment, the green dashboard light lighting up his face, showing his features in a way I had never seen them before. Gene handsome in the green light, maybe more handsome this evening than ever before, and interested in my story, in me.

This is the story I told Gene.

"It's like a picture in my mind," I said. I was looking at my lap, picking a callus on my hand. "What I remember is Ma standing in the moonlight, moonlight reflecting off the Butler Bins behind her. Ma was taunting Dad. She threw her head back and laughed at him. Laughed at him."

"How come she was standing out in the moonlight?"

"It was late, and she came to the door of the bunkhouse where Dad slept naked in the big bed. I was in the cot. They thought I was asleep, I guess, but I wasn't."

"How old were you when this happened?"

"It was about three years ago, I think, so I was ten, nine or ten, I think."

Dashes of white line on the road caught in the headlights, disappeared in front of us, erased by the pickup, *click, click, click* going through my mind as the dashes vanished.

"So you were about ten. She came to the door."

"Ma asked Dad to come outside to talk. She whispered,

but it was loud. Dad got up and pulled on his Levi's and went outside, barefoot, no shirt on.

"Ma held her quilted robe tight around her breasts with her arms, a few inches of her nightgown showed between the bottom of her robe and her ankles. She stood stiff on the gravel yard, her mouth set. She was angry.

"I could see them both through the bunkhouse window—Ma facing me, Dad's back turned my way, square shoulders, strong neck, his pants hanging low around his hips.

"Ma used her arms now as she talked. She pounded her hands together, pointing and jabbing with her finger. She leaned in toward my father, talking loud. I could hear her."

I looked out the pickup window. There was nothing to see in the darkness. The night was quiet, the only sound the pickup engine and tires on pavement.

"So what did she say?"

"She said, 'What in the hell were you thinking about?' to my father. She said, 'A neighbor girl, a kid with no experience, innocent, and all you can think of is playing around with her, diddling her for your excitement. Your pleasure.'

"There was a long quiet time when neither Dad nor Ma spoke. Dad looked away, across the yard, moonlight shining dull on the gravel, reflecting on the Butler Bins. Then Ma said, 'Her family from the Old Country, still thinking like they're in the Old Country, thinking like they're still in the goddamned Azores. Does she have a place to go? Does she have anywhere to turn? Does she even have a boyfriend to marry, to blame it on, for Christ's sake? Hell no, she doesn't. Marie doesn't let those girls out of the house at night without old Mrs. Moro going along. So how is Teresa going to explain being pregnant? Huh?'

"Ma stood back from Dad a bit. Dad didn't answer. He was looking at her. He moved his hands in front of him, open, palms up. Stepped toward her. Shook his head.

"What Ma said next, I don't know. She said it softly, her head turned sideways, said something in a taunting way to my father and then she laughed. She threw her head back. Laughed loud and slapped her thighs."

"What did your father do?"

"His hands curled into fists."

"And your mother?"

"She moved back close to Dad's face and she hissed words at him. Dad held his fists at his waist for a moment, then raised his arms. He stopped. But my mother didn't. She threw her head back, laughing again, and Dad swung his fist and hit my mother's jaw, and she sort of jumped backward with the force and she fell backward and rolled over on the gravel."

I couldn't say anything more.

I saw that Gene and I were dropping down a long grade into Livermore Valley. We were going faster again. I could make out trees and farm buildings when the Studebaker rounded a corner and the headlights shone on them. Out across the valley the lights of Livermore stretched in lines that were streetlights and lights in houses along them.

I mentioned the lights to Gene and looked at them for a long time so that he would think I was just interested in Livermore and not wiping my face.

"Did you talk to your mom or dad that night?"

"No. Dad was coming back to the bunkhouse then and I got into the cot. He put his boots and shirt on, took a coat from the hook, and left. Ma was gone when I got back to the window."

Gene was looking at me, concern showing all over his face. He slowed the pickup down and reached over and grabbed my shoulder.

"You feeling okay, Ace? Carsick? Need to get out and walk around a bit, get some fresh air?"

"No, I'm okay."

"Drink of water? Or something else—a Coke, maybe?"

"I'm fine," I said.

"Speak up if you need something," Gene said.

Every once in a while I caught him turn and glance at me. We rode across the Livermore Valley without talking, each of us quiet, thinking about the story of my mother and father, I guess. I felt good about telling the story to Gene. Gene was the right person to trust with the story.

Across the seat I watched Gene in the yellow-green light of the dashboard, his arm reaching to the steering wheel, his new wine-colored vest rounding over his shoulder, resting over his chest, dropping loose to his waist. Every once in a while the bright light of oncoming traffic lit things up and cast moving shadows around the cab where shadow wouldn't usually be. Gene was still handsome, though, especially handsome in the night light of the Studebaker cab.

What I remember then is starting the long climb out of the Livermore Valley through the dry grassy hills, amber in the daytime, black now at night, mostly invisible at night, and then I don't remember any more. I don't remember going over the hills, the hills I love the most on this ride, don't remember going down the hills on the other side into Tracy, crossing the flat farmland, tomatoes, sugar beets, don't remember the bridge at the Mossdale Y crossing the San Joaquin River.

Next thing I remember is Gene saying, "Home again." And me with my head against Gene's shoulder, my face resting on his shirt, hoping to God I hadn't drooled all over Gene's new shirt.

The Edge of the Road

 WHEN I WOKE UP THE NEXT morning—after the trip to Luther Burbank's garden, to San Francisco—my bedroom was bright with sunlight. I was thankful my mother hadn't come upstairs to wake me. I thought she must be doing things quietly in the kitchen to let me sleep late. Or maybe she was outside already, watering the garden.

I lay in bed for a while feeling warm in the sunshine, watching the sunshine reflect off the mirror over the dresser and bounce bright colors off the beveled edge onto the wall. I lay under the sheets, feeling my body with the flat of my hands, running my hands over my body, squeezing the muscle over my chest, feeling the muscle of my thighs, squeezing there, too, feeling my shoulders to see if they had grown.

When I got downstairs to the kitchen, it was bright with sunlight, too. Ma was in the kitchen and she asked if I wanted some bacon and eggs.

"Sure," I said.

"Do you want potatoes, too?"

"Sure."

Ma didn't say, What did you do on the trip? Or, How late was it when you got home? She didn't ask, Did you spend all the money I gave you? My mom didn't ask those questions.

"Did you have a good time?" she said. She stood in front of the stove and cracked two eggs into a frying pan, put the toast down in the toaster.

"I had a great time, Ma."

"That's good."

That's all she said about it. Ma never asked me anything more about the trip to Luther Burbank's garden. Made me want to tell her every little thing that happened, but I didn't. I knew I had the best mom there ever was.

It was ten o'clock before I started spading the perennial bed—what was going to be the perennial bed—when Gene drove up in his old pickup. Gene went into the kitchen to talk with Ma for a bit, I guess, and then he came out to where I was working.

"Hard at it, I see," Gene said.

"More or less."

"Well, it looks like a good job."

Gene took a brown paper bag from under his arm where he held it wedged next to his chest.

"Here," he said. "This is for you." I recognized the bag Gene got the day before at the City Lights Bookstore.

"For me?" I didn't really need to ask that question, he just said it was for me, but it came out before I thought about it.

I pushed the shovel into the ground with my foot and Gene and I walked over to the stairs by the back porch and sat down there side by side, bumping shoulders. I reached into the bag and pulled out a book—no surprise, if Gene got it at the City Lights. But I thought it would have writing in it, that it would tell a story, but it didn't.

I ran my hands over the book covers; the heavy-grained black paper felt like leather. Along the outside edge of the pages were half-moon dents with the letters of the alphabet showing. Put my finger on D and flipped it open to a blank lined page.

"It's a plant log. You can write down plant names as you learn them," Gene said. "Everything from *Acacia baileyana* to *Zelkova serrata*. Just write it down, make notes on how the plant grows, what it needs—sun or shade, wet or dry, stuff like that. You might want to make a note of where you saw the plant, so you can go back and have a second look if necessary."

I wanted to hug Gene right then, right there on the back porch steps, for giving me something so thoughtful, but I didn't. I slapped my hand down on the plant log where I had it sitting on my thigh.

"Thanks," I said.

Gene was looking at me. I wanted to tell him how I felt, but didn't know how. Didn't know how to say thanks for treating me like an adult, for trusting me to record the things he told me, didn't know how to tell him of other feelings I had, didn't understand the feelings or know what to call them, all tied up inside.

"Thanks a lot," I said. "This is great."

Gene smiled. I guess he understood. I hope he understood.

After Gene left, I went back to spading the perennial bed. That's where I was when I saw my father's Chevy flatbed truck turn into our driveway off Mariposa Road, curve past the black walnut tree, *Juglans nigra*, and pull up in front of the barn where my mother parks her car. I hadn't seen my dad since the morning Ma and I left the ranch, and I hadn't expected to see him now, here at the Home Place. I went over to the side porch where the truck was parked and went up the stairs onto the porch.

It was not my father I saw, it was my brother, Brad. He had driven my father's flatbed truck into town. What I saw just inside the porch, in the room my mother calls the parlor, was Ma hugging Brad. Ma had her arms around Brad tight and he bent over, rested his head on her shoulder. His hair had grown long, over his ears.

From the screened-in part of the porch where I stood I saw Brad's shoulders shake and Ma rock him back and forth the way she used to do when we were little kids and crying. I didn't go further into the house. I stayed on the screened-in porch, leaned my back against the side of the house that was the wall of the parlor, and let my chin rest on my chest. From there I heard Brad cry. He sobbed like he couldn't get breath.

Tears came to my eyes and I thought I might sit down. I moved away instead, walked back out the screened porch, careful not to let the door slam, and I took my shovel out to spade, to pretend I'd been spading all along.

It took spading awhile before I realized I was angry at Brad for being here, angry at Ma for holding him. Why did he have to horn in on what we were doing, on our lives? After spading, though, breaking up clods, I realized Brad needed our mother, too, needed to be held like that or he wouldn't be here, wouldn't be here crying and being held, crying and hugging not a regular part of my brother's way of acting.

I pretended to spade the soil for a while and then acted like I was cleaning the shovel, as if I take such good care of tools. Then I went back onto the side porch and banged the door hard and took off my boots before going into the kitchen in my stocking feet. Ma and Brad were sitting at the kitchen table, Brad drinking milk and eating a cookie and Ma having another cup of coffee.

"How you doing?" I noticed Brad's pants and shirt were dirty.

"Fine," he said. "How about you?"

"I'm doing pretty good." I wanted to tell Brad about my trip to Santa Rosa and San Francisco. But that could wait. I took a cookie from the plate.

"How's Dad?" I asked.

"He's okay."

Ma took a quick look at Brad. He finished his glass of milk and set it down before him, twirling it on the table between his hands.

"The harvester broke down, so I came to town to get some parts at Mott Brothers. Thought I'd stop and say hi to you two. See how you're doing," Brad said, like he was on top of everything, and I might have believed him if I hadn't seen him crying and hugging my mother.

"Hey, Ma," Brad said. "Can I have a cup of coffee instead of this stuff?" He pushed the empty milk glass toward the center of the table.

"Help yourself," Ma said.

"I'll get it." I went to the cupboard and got a thick white mug, poured it full of coffee at the stove, and brought it to my brother.

"I better go. Dad'll wonder what's keeping me. Better get going," Brad said, his just-filled mug of coffee in front of him.

He kept saying he was leaving, but continued to sit at the table after he finished his coffee. He took another cookie.

Ma got up and went to the Ovaltine jar in the cupboard and took out a bill and folded it over and over.

"Here, take this and get yourself a haircut. Stop at Abe Corn's and get a nice haircut. Keep what's left over. Buy something you'd like."

Brad looked down as he took the folded bill and put it in his pocket. He turned away and walked toward the side door. As he walked he hiked up his Levi's; he was tall and thin, no hips to hold his pants, wide belt or no.

Ma and I walked out on the porch with him, the screen door slammed behind us. The three of us walked to the side of the flatbed truck and Brad got in the driver's seat.

"Boy, you two have sure fixed Granny's place up," he said. "What made you paint the house this color, Ma?"

"I just liked it," she said.

"I liked the name," I said. "Taupe. You ever heard of taupe before? How many people you know live in a taupe-colored house?" I asked my brother.

"Just you two, I guess."

I was working on lightening up the situation a little. Ma had her hand around the frame that held the sideview mirror on the truck cab. I wondered if she was going to hang on to it when my brother drove out.

"Looks like you've been gardening, too," Brad said. "New trees and shrubs everywhere around here. Place looks good. Well, I've got to go."

Brad shifted the truck into reverse and began to move slowly backward and my mother let go of the sideview mirror, but she walked along beside the truck and then she raised her arm in the air and started waving as my brother turned the truck around and headed toward the road.

Before I could say anything to Ma, she grabbed up her apron and held it over her face and walked real fast to the back steps, almost ran to the back steps, and then she ran across the porch into the house.

I watched until Brad turned onto the road past the black walnut tree and headed toward Stockton, where he was going to Mott Brothers for parts to repair the harvester, and to Abe Corn's barbershop to get a haircut.

I walked slowly into the kitchen after Dad's truck disappeared around the corner by the Pasacco girls' place, but Ma wasn't in the kitchen. I walked through the house to the living room and from there I could hear her crying in the front bedroom.

I went to the door of the front bedroom and listened for a little while. Listened to Ma, and then I knocked gently on the door. No answer. I couldn't hear crying anymore.

"Is there something I can do?"

"No, I'm okay. It was just a surprise, seeing Brad. I'm okay. I'm going to rest a minute, gather my agates, that's all. You go on with what you're doing."

I didn't, though. I didn't go on with what I was doing, I went up the back stairs to where my bedroom was and I closed the door and lay down on my bed and cried, too. I pulled the pillow up onto my chest and rolled over and curled up holding the pillow and I cried.

That's how I was when I got the bright idea. Got the

bright idea to spend some time with my brother and go out to the ranch to see Dad.

I wrote Ma a note that said I was going for a walk, said I wasn't sure where I was going but I'd be back for dinner. I left the note on the kitchen table. Then I stood in the living room and listened for sounds of my mother in the front bedroom. I couldn't hear her.

"Ma," I said softly. "I'm going out for a while. I'll be back for dinner."

"Okay," she said. "Be back for dinner."

I walked out the gravel driveway to the shoulder of Mariposa Road and sat down by the mailbox and waited for Brad to come back from getting parts at Mott Brothers, and from getting a haircut.

I sat there about twenty minutes with my back propped against the mailbox, watching the road from Stockton, before I saw Dad's truck round the corner by the Pasacco girls' place. I stood up and brushed off my Levi's. I moved out to the road where the blacktop met the gravel shoulder and waved my arm up and down like a railroad brakeman.

From where I stood I could see Brad sitting in the truck cab behind the steering wheel, but I wasn't sure he saw me. Then I heard him begin to double-clutch, shifting down, acting like he was a professional trucker on a long haul.

Brad reached over his head, and the signal arm outside the truck cab rose straight in the air. My brother was turning off the road, stopping to pick me up.

The tires of the truck kicked up dust as Brad pulled onto the shoulder. I ran along beside the truck until it stopped. Brad was halfway to the intersection of Pock Lane when I caught up to the door and jumped onto the running board, pulled the door open and climbed into the cab beside him.

"Where do you think you're going?" Brad stared at me.

I sat in the shotgun seat and stared at my brother, not because of what he said, but because of how he looked. Brad had gone to Abe Corn's barbershop like my mother told him to, but instead of getting a regular haircut, he'd gotten a flattop burr.

"You trying to look like President Eisenhower?" I said.

Brad leaned way over toward me and looked at himself in the rearview mirror. He ran his open hand gently over his bristly hair.

"What's it to you?" he said. Then he looked at me with a wide smile and said, "Ike never had it so good."

"Neither did Mamie," I said. We had a good laugh on Ike and Mamie.

Brad rubbed his hand across his thigh to get rid of the grease from his hair. There was an open brown bag on the seat between us, a jar of peach pomade inside.

Springs beneath the leather seat poked me in a couple of places; I scrunched around to get comfortable. The seat on the driver's side had a saddle blanket over it where the leather was worn out.

"Thought I'd ride out to the ranch with you for a visit," I said. "Spend some time with you and Dad."

"Ma know you're going?"

"I told her I was going out for a while."

The truck was rolling again. Brad concentrated on shifting the truck into higher gear, leaving his hand on the gearshift knob between us, working the clutch pedal, the gas. He looked out the rearview mirror. I had one arm over the back of the seat, my other arm rested on the open window. I watched my brother.

"Things aren't like they used to be out on the ranch," Brad said. We looked at each other across the seat.

"What do you mean?"

There was a long quiet spell.

"What things aren't like they used to be?" I asked.

"I don't know." He paused, then said, "It's just, things are different since Ma left. That's all. Things change, I guess. That's all."

Brad released the lever above his head and lowered the signal to the side of the truck. I put my feet on a lug box that held three new sprockets, a box of lock washers, and a box of cotter keys.

"Dad's different?" I said. "Has he changed?"

"Well, yeah, he's changed—not so much he's changed, more changed how he acts, does stuff he never used to do."

Brad signaled and we turned left off Mariposa Road onto Farmington Road, Route 4. We passed Montezuma School, where my mother had gone to grammar school and her mother had gone to grammar school, too.

"What's he do?" I asked. "What stuff? He giving you the silent treatment all the time?"

"Most of the time." Brad laughed. "The whole damn thing is like silent treatment, worse than the silent treatment. It's like I'm not even there, or if I'm there, I'm just another hired man."

A mile east of Montezuma School we slowed down to cross a wide stretch of bare dirt where construction workers were building a new Highway 99. The new four-lane highway was finished between Fresno and Bakersfield; now they were working on the link between Modesto and Sacramento.

The El Rancho Motel was gone. A huge mound of dirt that was the beginning of the Farmington Road overpass sat where the motel used to be as if the El Rancho had never been there. I couldn't believe it.

Brad picked up speed and we approached the Southern Pacific Railroad crossing, doing forty-five miles an hour at least. The railroad crossing was a quick rise and drop in the flat land, and my stomach flipped over as Brad sped over the crossing. The truck rattled and bounced; sprockets in the lug box clanked.

Brad looked my way. "Got ya, huh?"

"Yeah, a bit." I liked the feeling. Smiled.

Brad and I rode along without saying anything for several miles, my arm resting on the window opening, feeling the breeze on my hand and face. I watched out the window as we passed a row of Osage orange trees planted along the edge of the Hollenback place. Wondered what Gene Tole would call Osage orange trees. Thought about Gene a bit, daydreamed him digging potatoes, then standing on the porch of his cottage, leaning against the roof support post, wearing a white T-shirt, smiling. A car waiting to pull out of Hollenback's driveway brought me back.

When I was a little kid, Dad told me about Charlie Hollenback, who'd been his best friend when they were boys. I thought about the picture of Charlie Hollenback in our oldest family picture album, the picture of Charlie taken when he was sixteen, graduating from high school. My father never went to high school. That summer when he was sixteen Charlie got sick with spinal meningitis and died three days later. My father lost his best friend. That's the story Dad told me about the Hollenbacks.

I wondered how Mr. and Mrs. Hollenback felt when their son, Charlie, died in three days. I wondered how my mother and father would feel if I died.

Brad reached up to the sun visor over the windshield and pulled a pack of Pall Mall cigarettes from behind it. He shook a couple cigarettes to the end of the pack and pulled one out with his lips. He held the pack toward me, I shook my head.

Brad took a book of paper matches from behind the cellophane wrapper of the Pall Malls and pulled a match loose, held the match pack with his hand still on the steering wheel, and with the other hand he struck the match and lit the cigarette. He pulled his breath in and let go a stream of bright smoke. Brad waved the match back and forth, and when the flame was out he tossed the match from the window on his side and put the matches and the cigarettes back above the sun visor.

I watched my brother; Brad had his smoking technique down perfect. I wanted to ask him how many hours he spent in front of a mirror to get so good. I wanted to say, You don't have to try so hard, to my brother. But I let it go.

"I moved out to the bunkhouse," Brad said.

"How come?"

"It's part of what's changed. Dad goes out at night all the time. Mostly he goes over to the House of Blue Lights on Duncan Road, I think."

I knew the House of Blue Lights, a barn converted to a dance hall and beer joint. Blue neon lights outlined the roof and windows of the barn, and blue neon lights spelled out HOUSE OF BLUE LIGHTS across the side. At night the lights shone bright and eerie out in the country with nothing but flat farmland all around. Dad had talked about the House of Blue Lights, saying it was an awful place. Nothing but Okies and losers go there, he said. One and the same, he said.

"He comes home in the middle of the night and wakes me up," Brad said. "Stuff like that. Wants to talk, wants to argue. He started coming home with other people and I decided to move to the bunkhouse. It's cleaner out there anyway."

"Dad? What other people does he come home with?"

"Different people. Women. Different women. Now it's

just Violet, though. Violet has kind of, well, moved in. She has a trailer house parked behind the house; there's no toilet or shower in it, though, so she's always in the house taking a powder," Brad said. "But at least when they fuck, they mostly fuck in the trailer house."

"They what?"

"They fuck," Brad said. "*Fuck!*"

Brad stubbed the butt of his cigarette out on the metal dashboard and flicked the butt out the window. He ran his hand over his bristly hair.

I couldn't believe Brad said what he said, couldn't believe what he just said about my father was true.

The truck rolled across the wooden bridge over the Mormon Slough, the bridge whitewashed white, two-by-twelve planks rumbling as we rode over them.

I didn't know what *fuck* meant, exactly, not like my brother just used it; it meant having sex, I knew that much, but having sex meant being in love, meant being married.

My brother let up on the gas pedal just before we got to Berger's place. Elva Berger was out front dragging a garden hose with a lawn sprinkler on it around her yard. Brad and I waved. Elva waved back.

"That kookie religious bitch," Brad said.

"She been trying to convert you?" I asked. My brother ignored me.

Brad double-clutched and put out the signal for us to turn right, turn off Farmington Road onto Jack Tone Road. In the distance, three quarters of a mile down Jack Tone

Road, I could see the walnut orchard, the windmill, and the tank house, dry flat field of barley in between.

All of a sudden, I didn't want to go to the ranch anymore. I couldn't figure out the things Brad had told me. How could Dad be in love with a woman named Violet, in love with a woman he'd met at the House of Blue Lights, having sex with her, fucking her?

Brad drove slow along Jack Tone Road. The road was narrow; no shoulder, and full of potholes. It seemed to me that we drove slower than usual, like the truck didn't really want to get back to the ranch.

Brad didn't bother to signal when he turned the truck right onto the gravel road past the mailbox, RT. 4 BOX 134 written in black letters on the side, RYAN, our family name, written in black letters, too. Two bullet holes through the mailbox, through our name, something new to me, where someone had taken target practice with our mailbox, our name.

We drove past the windmill, past where the garden used to be, and we curved around the slight rise in the land halfway between the road and the yard.

A pack of dogs ran toward us, different sizes and colors, all barking and jumping and running around the truck.

"Fucking mutts," Brad said.

"Where'd they come from?"

"They came with the bitch. A package deal, I guess."

"Five of them?"

"Six," Brad said. "With any luck one is under a wheel."

159

I looked across the seat at Brad; he was staring straight ahead. His jaw muscle flexed. He pulled the truck up in front of the shop and turned off the switch.

"I'm gonna drop the sprockets off," Brad said. "No telling where Dad is. Check around if you want to see him."

When I opened the truck door the dogs had stopped circling and were lining up to take a piss on the truck tires. Two of them put their paws up on the running board, sniffed, then dropped back down and milled around, barking some more. I got out of the truck cab and the dogs sniffed me, got bored and wandered off.

On my way to the house a cinnamon-colored dog came up to me. She was an older dog, a shorthair with only one eye, the empty eye socket sewn shut, a dent where the eye had been. I petted her neck as we walked toward the house.

"What's your name, girl?" I said.

I stroked her ear.

"What happened to your eye, girl?"

I had trouble looking at her. For some reason she bothered me; maybe it was that she didn't see everything, but what did I know—maybe she did. She walked close to me, her head next to my thigh as if she were my guide, her constant expression a wink.

Weeds grew tall in the area where my mother's clothesline had been, and morning-glory vines crowded out the Paul's Scarlet rose that climbed the arbor at the end of the picket fence around the house. Behind the house I saw

Violet's trailer parked with a big square block of wood in front of the door for a step.

I went up the stairs to the back door of our house, the only door into the house we ever used. It was odd what I did then: I knocked on the door. I had to do it.

No one came to the door. It was quiet everywhere, like the ranch was deserted, no one around, which wasn't true, I knew. Brad was out in the shop. I opened the door and went inside to the glassed-in back porch where my mother had her washing machine with the wringer she swung over the concrete wash trays when she did the wash. The porch was full of dirty clothes piled on the floor. The clothes were stale, smelled bad.

The glass windows that let in morning light and made the porch a nice place to be had been covered with big pieces of cardboard tacked to the wooden window frames. It felt like something was being hidden on the porch.

In the kitchen dirty dishes were stacked so high I couldn't see the drain board. The sink was full of used pans, and Ma's cast-iron frying pan sat rusting in dirty water.

I turned around to explore in the living room, when a woman holding a stained yellow terry-cloth bathrobe around her walked through the doorway.

"Who are you?" she asked. "Oh my God, you must be the other one."

She rewrapped the bathrobe higher and tighter around herself to keep her loose breasts from showing.

"Are you Violet?" I asked.

"Call me Vi, honey," she said.

She came over to me and pulled me to her breasts, which were showing more again since she quit holding the bathrobe.

"I'm here helping your daddy keep things going since you and your mama had to move to town. Helping cook and clean, helping Brad, but he doesn't need much help."

Vi giggled, like there was something funny about Brad not needing help. She sat down at the kitchen table and took a cigarette from a pack sitting on the table. She went to the kitchen stove, turned on a burner, and bent over to light the cigarette off the gas flame. She came back to the table and sat smoking the cigarette. Vi had reddish brown hair parted down the middle. White and dark brown hair showed where she parted it.

"I hope we can be friends, honey. Your daddy is real important to me. Real important. He's the sweetest thing. I just hang on his every word. Hang on every word of his, really I do."

Vi looked at me, then turned away, blew a puff of smoke and waved her hand back and forth through it as though she was concerned that I might breathe her cigarette smoke. Her loose breasts swung freely under the robe. I was afraid that her robe might fall free from her breasts and expose her nipples. At the same time, I hoped it would.

"We met over at the Blue Lights, your daddy and

me," she said. "The Maddox Brothers and Rose were there. Rose Maddox has a beautiful voice, I could listen to Rose Maddox sing all day, and your daddy . . . he can dance. Your daddy cuts a mighty wide swath on the dance floor, honey. Mighty wide swath. He's a sweetie, honey. I can't get enough of him."

Vi turned away and blew smoke, waved her hand.

"I mean I can't spend enough time with him, honey. That's all I mean to say. Next Saturday night Bill Monroe and the Country Gentlemen are going to be over at the Lights. Hope we can go, your daddy and me. Your daddy is a sweetheart, he's all the country gentleman I need."

There were footsteps on the porch and Brad came into the kitchen.

"Brad, honey, what on earth happened to your hair?" Vi stood up and went over to my brother and ran her hand lightly over his hair.

"I got it cut, Vi," Brad said. "What happened to yours?" He laughed.

"Your brother's such a card." Vi looked over her shoulder at me, giggled, then pretended to be hurt. "A real cutup, he is. That's what I like about your brother. That's one thing I like about him. This haircut is another." She stood close to my brother, her robe loose, and ran her hand over his hair.

"Where'd you get the haircut, Son?" My father stood in the doorway to the porch. He surprised me. I think he surprised Vi and Brad, too.

Vi moved away from Brad and sat back down at the kitchen table. She stubbed out her cigarette in a saucer, pulled her robe tight.

"Abe Corn's," Brad said.

My father went to the icebox and took a glass bottle of ice water out. He unscrewed the lid and took a long drink of water directly from the bottle. His Adam's apple bobbed up and down as he drank. The beginning of a beard made Dad's face look dark. He put the lid back on the water bottle and wiped his mouth across his sleeve. He opened the icebox door and set the bottle back on the shelf.

"I thought Abe Corn knew better than to give a haircut like that." Dad spoke in a low voice.

"Hi, Dad," I said. "Thought I'd come out for a visit."

My father continued to look at Brad.

"Where'd you get the money to pay for a haircut?"

"From Ma." I could hardly hear Brad, his head was bent down so low.

Dad took a red bandanna handkerchief out of his back pocket and blew his nose. He made a loud noise, took a long time to wipe his nose, carefully fold the handkerchief, and put it back in his pocket.

"That stinks," Dad said. "That really stinks, the haircut stinks, the whole fucking thing stinks."

My father went toward Brad.

"Son of mine taking money from a woman, for a fucking haircut like that." Dad put the flat of his hand on my brother's chest and shoved him backward.

My father stepped forward, following Brad.

"Took money from your mother for a fucking haircut? A haircut like that?"

"It wasn't his idea, Dad," I said.

"Shut up, houseboy." Dad didn't look at me. "Mama's boy. You. Always a mama's boy."

"Sweetheart, don't get all upset." Vi stood up. "Please, don't."

"I don't like you taking money from your ma. I don't like it one fucking bit," Dad said. He grabbed a pot and hurled it against the splashboard behind the sink. The pot clattered off the drain board and landed on the floor.

My father made quick punching strikes at Brad with his fist, hitting Brad on the shoulder. Brad fell backward slightly from the force of the punches. His hands were by his side, fingers spread open wide.

"What's the matter?" Dad asked. He punched my brother again. "Come on," he said. "Come on."

Brad looked right in my father's face. My father pushed again on Brad's chest with his open hand. My brother was against the kitchen sink now. Dad swung his fist again, hitting Brad in the stomach. A stack of plates and saucers fell off the drain board to the floor and shattered. Dad stood back, watched my brother as he tried to straighten up. Tried to draw breath.

"Ready?" my father said. His fists up.

Brad straightened up, his hands open. He looked at my father. Shook his head.

"Think about it when you go begging for money." Dad turned and went into the living room, like he was going to relax, going to read the newspaper.

Brad walked to the back porch, the screen door slammed. I looked at Vi. She followed my father into the living room, and I went outside after my brother.

From the back steps, I saw Brad running through the walnut orchard, visible, invisible, visible again, running through the trees, weaving through the white-barked branches of the trees. Brad ran toward Little John Creek. I started to follow him, but stopped. I stopped at the edge of the walnut orchard where the soil had been disked and planed. Brad didn't want me there. Didn't want to talk with me brother to brother, didn't want me to see what I'd already seen.

When I got to the shop I washed my face in cold water from the faucet, dried my face on my shirt. I started walking out the gravel road past where the garden used to be, past the windmill, out to Jack Tone Road. The cinnamon short-hair dog with one eye walked beside me, her head near my thigh. She stopped when I got to the road and sat back on her haunches, her head high, watching me with one eye as I started walking along Jack Tone Road.

The sun was bright in the west, several hours of sunlight left before dark. Not enough sunlight left to get back to the Home Place before dark, though; no way to get back to the Home Place in time for supper.

Walking a long time, not yet to Farmington Road, not even to Farmington Road, only two miles to the corner, Stockton, the Home Place, twenty miles more.

I turned onto Farmington Road, headed toward Stockton, walked past Berger's place, the water sprinkler on the end of the hose twirling slowly, casting water on the lawn where Elva Berger had left it. I walked another quarter mile, almost to Sharp's place, on the right, when a car came behind me.

Elva Berger passed me in her DeSoto, going hardly faster than I was walking, and then she pulled over, off the road. I opened the door and looked inside.

"I'm going to Stockton for evening meeting," Elva said. "Want a ride?"

"Yes, Mrs. Berger," I said. "I'd really like a ride." I slid onto the polished leather seat of Elva Berger's big old DeSoto and she pulled back on the road to Stockton, never going more than thirty-five miles an hour the whole trip. Slowed to ten miles per hour to go over the Southern Pacific Railroad crossing, no flip in the stomach this time. But it was faster riding with Elva than when I was walking. That much is for sure.

When I got to the Home Place my mother was in the kitchen pounding meat with a mean-looking hammer.

"Swiss steak. Sound good?" she said.

"Sure does," I said.

"So," Ma said. "How were things out on the ranch?"

I guess I looked pretty stunned. I didn't say anything.

"Elva Berger called. Said you were walking by there. Asked if she should give you a ride. I just figured."

Ma washed her hands and dried them on her apron. She came over to the table where I was sitting and sat down. She looked at me and said, "How was it out there?"

We sat at the table, Ma and I, for a long time and I told her about everything I'd seen at the ranch. Told about Brad's haircut, about Vi, the House of Blue Lights, about Dad hitting Brad. Told about Brad running through the walnut orchard toward Little John Creek, and about the cinnamon-colored dog with one eye that walked me to the edge of the road.

Red
River

 ON SATURDAY MORNING I WENT
outside after breakfast, planning to work in the garden. But I
didn't do a lick of work. I took a glass of orange juice with me
and I wandered around in the garden looking at the plants,
scuffing my feet on the pea-gravel paths, rattling gravel. I
thought, and I drank orange juice.

Thought about what I could do to help Brad, help my
father, my mother, and myself. But no helpful thoughts
came. Thoughts that did come got blurry right away and
were useless.

I set the empty orange juice glass down on the bench
in the herb garden and walked out into the open field toward
the Pasacco girls' place. It felt good to be alone, away from
the house. I sat down in the tall grass and lay back flat where

no one could see me. I was looking at the sky, watching clouds, trying to make out cloud pictures, when I heard someone coming in the grass. I rolled over on my stomach to look. It was Parkie.

"Hi," Parkie said. "I saw you walking out here, so I came over to say hi. Hi," he said.

I just looked at him. I thought about telling him I wanted to be alone, thought about saying, Okay, you've said hi, now why don't you leave. But I didn't.

"What's new?" he said. "I'm glad I saw you."

Parkie sat down beside me, laid back in the grass. Rolls of fat around his stomach jiggled.

"I came looking for you," Parkie said. "Know what? I've got my sister's car tomorrow night. Want to go to the movies? Want to see John Wayne in *Red River*? It's on downtown, at the Ritz. I really want to see it. My sister said I could use her car. Want to go?"

"Well, sure," I said. "I'll have to ask, but I'm sure it's okay."

"Good," Parkie said. "I'm glad to have a friend. I've been trying to shake this girl. She's been after me. I liked her at first, then she got to be too much. She really fell hard for me, head over heels. A couple dates and she thought she owned me. Got all clingy. I couldn't shake her."

"Is that right?" He was talking like he'd been vaccinated with a phonograph needle.

"Sure is. Diane Davis. She's a sophomore. Fell head over heals for me, like a ton of bricks. What could I do? Phoning me all the time. Wanting to go out. Want to see her picture?"

Parkie jerked back and forth a couple times, then heaved onto his side and sat up. Parkie's T-shirt edged up and his pants slipped down. A roll of white skin showed around his middle. The crack of his butt appeared when he bent forward to dig for his wallet. Parkie thumbed through a picture holder and held the wallet toward me, his finger holding the folder open to a black-and-white school photo.

"That's her," Parkie said. "What do you think? Quite a number, huh? She's crazy about me. She's okay, I just got tired of her."

"She looks nice," I said, which was true. Diane Davis had a huge grin, pixie haircut, and eyes that were squinted shut by her grin and her thick glasses.

"I couldn't take it anymore."

Parkie threw a dirt clod into the open field, like the umpire of a baseball game after he yells "Play ball."

"I wrote Diane a postcard that I was going to be in San Diego with my brother and his wife the rest of the summer. I put the postcard in an envelope with a note telling my brother to put the postcard in the mail there. I'm off the hook. No phone calls, no whining—not for the rest of the summer, anyway. Pretty slick, huh?"

"Why didn't you just tell her you didn't want to see her for a while?"

Parkie stared at me, not believing what he'd heard me say.

"I couldn't do that to her. I just couldn't break her heart like that," he said.

Late Sunday afternoon I was sitting on the front steps waiting for Parkie to come pick me up for the movies, to see *Red River*, when my mother came out on the porch.

"That was Dexter Parkinson on the phone," she said. "He said he's going to be late."

"He's already late," I said.

"Said he couldn't find the keys to his sister's car," Ma said. "I guess he finally got one from his mother. It was a complicated story. Confusing."

"I'll bet," I said.

I began to think I'd made a mistake saying I'd go to the movies with Parkie.

Ma went back inside the house. I sat on the steps and watched cars going by on the road.

After just a few minutes I saw a pink Nash Rambler that looked like an upside-down bathtub with wheels on the bottom speeding toward our driveway. Parkie sat low in the driver's seat and looked out through the circle of the steering wheel. He gripped the steering wheel tight with both hands and aimed the Rambler at the driveway. He didn't move his hands to turn the steering wheel; instead, he banked his whole body over at a forty-five-degree angle, like he was riding a motorcycle.

"I'm off, Ma," I hollered through the screen door. I ran down the steps and got into Parkie's sister's inverted bathtub with wheels.

"There's still time to drag Main Street," Parkie said.

"Why bother?" I said.

It wasn't Friday night, wasn't Saturday night, it was Sunday afternoon, for crying out loud.

"What's the point?" I said.

The point was, though, that Parkie was driving, and when we got to downtown Stockton, he drove along Main Street, two-lane traffic going the same direction. We passed JC Penney's, passed the Ritz Theater with a young woman sitting in the fancy shell out front selling tickets to a few people going to see *Red River*. Neon lights around the front of the Ritz Theater were lit. It didn't make much sense; the sun was still bright and the neon light disappeared.

In the next block the driver in the car behind us began to honk the horn.

"What's with that jerk?" Parkie said loudly. The man in the car behind us honked again and Parkie reared up and glared out the back window.

"Asshole!" Parkie hollered, and flung his arm over the backseat, directing the driver to go around us. The driver honked again, and this time Parkie rolled down the window, thrust his arm in the air, and jabbed his hand up and down.

"What are you doing?" I said.

"Flagging this asshole the bird, what do you think?" Parkie said.

"The bird?" I said.

"You're hopeless," Parkie said.

"Your not showing a whole lot of promise yourself," I said.

The car behind us pulled up next to my side of the pink Rambler. The driver hung his arm out the window.

"Your keys are in the trunk latch," he said. He pointed and grinned.

"Thanks," I said, and waved.

The man waved back, turned to the woman sitting next to him, said something. They both laughed as they drove away.

"Shit," Parkie said.

Parkie slammed the Rambler to a stop in the middle of Main Street and opened the door. He stood beside the Rambler a minute and hiked up his pants. He walked around the car like he was someone important, like leaving the keys in the trunk of the car was exactly what he had intended to do all along.

I stared straight ahead through the windshield as though everything was normal. I acted like the traffic light was red instead of green. Acted like we were moving along in traffic instead of blocking it, acted like people behind us were not honking, not hollering out their windows.

Parkie got the keys out of the trunk latch, hiked up his

pants again, and stood in the middle of Main Street waving to the people in cars behind us like he was running for mayor, part of a parade. He ran back around the car still waving.

I was bent down, carefully, slowly retying my shoes, when Parkie opened the door and got in the driver's seat.

The only light in the theater came from the PREVIEWS OF COMING ATTRACTIONS on the screen. Parkie and I stood just inside the red velvet curtain separating the lobby from the theater while our eyes adjusted.

The MovieTone Newsreel came on and made enough light for us to find seats in the middle of the theater. Parkie ate popcorn he'd gotten at the snack bar, drank Coca-Cola, rattling ice in the paper cup. I ate popcorn, too.

In the MovieTone Newsreel Queen Elizabeth II of England got off an airplane in Kenya and waved to her subjects. The Queen and her husband, Prince Philip, were in Kenya to start giving the country of Kenya back to the people who lived there.

When evening came the Queen and Prince were at a banquet in their honor. The banquet was held outside under a huge tent. Queen Elizabeth and Prince Philip were dressed up—jewels on her, medals on him—sitting in front of a crowd of African people. The African people wore exotic robes and feathers and beads. They were sweating in the hot evening air.

It was strange. The Queen and Prince sitting up straight,

surrounded by all those black people. The Queen and Prince looked like the whitest people in the world, and I couldn't figure out how they'd learned not to sweat.

The newsreel switched to a story about soldiers in Korea; the film followed the soldiers on patrol, guarding the 42nd parallel, making everything safe for the South Korean people. After the patrol the newsreel showed the soldiers in their barracks, making their bunks, eating in a mess hall and playing pool at the base exchange. The newsreel showed the soldiers getting letters from home, which seemed kind of sad to me, but then the soldiers went on rest and relaxation in Australia and that didn't look so tough.

Red River came on then. Boy, what happened in *Red River*, at the end of the cattle drive, it was too much, I wasn't ready for it, movie make-believe got too real for me.

See, what happened was John Wayne raised Montgomery Clift like his own son, and when Montgomery Clift was grown, they got in a fight over a cattle drive, and John Wayne, who was a tough guy, got too tough, and said he was going to kill Montgomery Clift when he caught up with him at the end of the cattle drive, even though John Wayne was like Montgomery Clift's father.

When John Wayne caught up with Montgomery Clift in Abilene at the end of the cattle drive, after Joanne Dru had fallen in love with Montgomery Clift, John Wayne found Montgomery Clift in a dusty street and started hitting him. It was just like my father and Brad, Montgomery Clift not fighting back against John Wayne and John Wayne pounding Montgomery Clift something terrible, and then John Wayne got his gun out of his holster and was about to shoot Montgomery Clift where he had fallen all beat up on the dirt street.

That's when Joanne Dru stepped in with a rifle and shot the gun out of John Wayne's hand and she gave both John Wayne and Montgomery Clift a lecture and said they were acting like a couple of schoolboys and that they should be ashamed of themselves. Montgomery Clift got up and John Wayne and Montgomery Clift fell over together into a cart full of pots and pans and they made this terrible racket and mess in the pots and pans, but they laughed and kind of helped each other out of the pile of pots and pans and junk that had been in the cart, and they were happy again like they'd been before the cattle drive.

It was too much, seeing John Wayne and Montgomery Clift fighting like my father and Brad, father fighting, son not fighting.

At the end I sat in the dark theater watching the characters in *Red River* ride back to their ranch in the southwest, Joanne Dru going along, too, while the sun was setting, and the music got loud, and the names of the people who helped make the movie went by too fast too read.

I was trying not to cry about John Wayne and Montgomery Clift, about my father and Brad.

Then it was bright lights, real world, and being snapped back to the Ritz Theater.

"Oh, shit!" Parkie said right into my ear. I looked at him.

"What's the matter?" I said.

"That's her. Right down there between those other two girls. Oh, shit."

I couldn't figure out what Parkie was talking about. The only "her" I could think of was Joanne Dru. Three girls near the front of the theater started walking up the aisle. Parkie was fishing in his jeans pocket. The jeans were tight, and he couldn't get his hand in the pocket. When he finally got his hand in his pocket, he pulled out some change and spilled it on the concrete floor, making a loud ringing sound.

Parkie slid off his chair onto the floor, the crack of his butt showing above his belt about like Mae West's chest showed in *My Little Chickadee*. Parkie began to search under the seat for the change he'd dropped. He crawled away from the aisle where the three girls were walking to leave the theater.

That's when I figured it out, when I saw the girl in the middle, short dark hair in a pixie cut, eyes squinted shut by her grin, her thick glasses. I rested the side of my head on the heel of my hand, my elbow on the armrest. With my other hand I scratched my pant leg like I was intent on getting a stain off my pants. The three girls looked at me, looked along the row of seats where Parkie crawled around after his change.

Diane Davis and her friends didn't seem to recognize Parkie, didn't act like they knew him. The girl who walked behind Diane and her friend looked at me and smiled like she wanted to be friends. I smiled back. I wondered if she thought I was with Parkie, with the kid crawling on the floor of the Ritz Theater.

There was no problem talking Parkie into going to the Gay Nineties pizza parlor after the movie.

"Ever had pizza?" I asked.

"What's pizza?" Parkie said.

"Great food," I said.

Parkie shifted the Rambler into high gear and headed for El Dorado Street, where the Gay Nineties pizza parlor was located across from Eden Square.

Parkie and I tried to see in the Gay Nineties the first time we walked past. The view through the plate glass window in front was blocked by wood shutters inside. Dark wood shutters covered the glass door, too.

"Do you think we belong in there?" Parkie said.

"Sure we do," I said.

"I've never been in a place like this before. It looks like a bar. My mother would kill me."

"It's okay," I said, after the second walk-by. "Let's go in."

"Okay, I'm with you all the way, buddy." Parkie talked like he was Walter Brennan and I was Montgomery Clift in *Red River*, and we were scouting Indians. I pulled the door open and walked in, Parkie like a shadow right behind me.

The Gay Nineties was long and narrow. Sawdust was sprinkled over the floor. An antique bar with glasses and mirrors was along one wall. The walls were old brick, unpainted and rough. I walked past the backs of men seated at the bar to a counter near the rear of the Gay Nineties, where I ordered a pizza with everything on it.

"No little fish," I said, remembering Gene Tole ordering at Mario's.

The young man behind the counter smiled, handed me a playing card, the Jack of Hearts.

"No little fish," he said. "Leave the card on your table. We'll bring your pizza over." I stood at the counter a moment, Parkie stood beside me, gawking.

"You pay at the bar," the young man said. "Order your drinks over there, too."

Parkie followed me to the bar and we ordered Coca-Colas and paid for the pizza. I looked in the bar mirror and saw wood tables with captain's chairs around them. Saw the rough brick wall, the dark-stained wood shutters over the window, soft light filtering through in streaks. Saw men and women sitting around the tables eating pizza pie, pouring beer from pitchers, drinking from steins, talking, laughing.

These men and women looked comfortable, happy. I believed the men and women in the Gay Nineties pizza parlor had interesting thoughts, told funny stories, enjoyed being together. I had a wish then. The wish was to be a part of this group of people, to belong among them, to fit in.

Still, I remembered what Gene Tole had said, so I told

Parkie that we should go upstairs to the balcony to wait for our pizza pie to be brought to us. Parkie and I were alone in the balcony. We sat at a table next to the wood rail and looked over the edge of the balcony and watched what was going on at the bar and the tables where the men and women sat and ate and talked.

"I bet there are communists in here," Parkie said. "I bet this place is crawling with communists."

"What exactly do you think a communist is going to do to you, Parkie? Wash your brain? You want to make a run for it while you still can?"

"No, no, this place is neat," Parkie said. "No kidding. It's neat here. I like this place."

The young man from the kitchen came up the stairs with our pizza pie.

"One of you guys the Jack of Hearts?" the young man said, smiling. His hair was cut in a burr like my brother Brad's.

"Oh, that's me," Parkie said.

The young man looked at Parkie.

"I don't think so. The Joker, maybe." The young man laughed and set the pizza pie between Parkie and me. He took paper napkins from the pocket in his apron and set them on the table.

"Are there communists in here?" Parkie said. The young man looked at Parkie for a moment, a blank expression on his face.

"The Joker, for sure," the young man said. He laughed again.

"I just want to know," Parkie said. "My mother would kill me."

"Hope you like the pizza," the young man said. "Watch out for any little fish—and the communists," he grinned.

Brad

 GENE TOLE ALWAYS SAID, "SOIL,
gardeners work with soil! Leave the dirt to the other folks.
Dirt is a different story altogether. I'll tell you about dirt
some other time."

I woke up that morning thinking about soil, thinking
about soil and the sand and manure that Gene and I had
spaded into the soil, into the perennial bed.

"I'll be over early in the morning," Gene had said. "With
a pickup load of perennials. We'll get them planted early
and water them in good before it gets too hot. They'll never
know they've been transplanted."

I heard voices downstairs in the kitchen. I couldn't make
out who it was talking with my mother, but I thought it
must be Gene having an early cup of coffee with her.

I got out of bed, pulled on my khaki cutoffs, and looked out the window. Dad's pickup truck was parked in the driveway. I couldn't imagine what my father would be doing at the Home Place this early in the morning, or at any time, for that matter. I pulled the cover up over my unmade bed and closed the bedroom door behind me.

But it wasn't my father. It was Brad. Downstairs in the kitchen Ma sat at the table with a mug of coffee between her hands listening to my brother. Ma was looking at her coffee mug, not saying much. Brad was excited and talking a lot.

Ma looked up. "Your brother has decided to join the Marine Corps."

"Marines?"

I thought of the billboard on East Main Street, thought of the blue pants with a red stripe on the leg, thought of the white cadet cap and a saber hanging from a belt. THE U.S. MARINE CORPS BUILDS MEN, the sign said. Then I thought of the young men in Korea I'd seen in the newsreel sitting around in a barracks in their underwear reading letters and playing cards.

"Marines? Why the Marines? How come?" I said.

"I've not decided to join, I've joined. I've done it. I'm in, leaving today," Brad said. "Going to Oakland on a bus. I'll be inducted in Oakland. Then I get orders, probably to Camp Pendleton, or maybe to some camp in South Carolina."

"South Carolina?" I said.

Ma stood up and went to the sink. She looked out the

window to the south where the perennial bed was ready to be planted. She ran hot and cold water into the sink, adjusting the handles to get the temperature she wanted. She poured dish-washing soap into the sink and swished her hand back and forth through the water to mix the soap and water, and then she lifted some dirty dishes into the sink and began to wash them.

She took the top dish off the stack and with a dishrag in her hand she moved her hand around and around the dish as if she had forgotten she was washing dishes, and then she set the dish down in the sink beside the sink with water in it, and she picked up another dish and moved her hand with the dishrag around and around on it.

I got up and went over to the icebox to get some orange juice, and then I went over to the sink to get a drinking glass and to look at Ma, which was what I really wanted to do all along, not get orange juice or get a glass to pour it into, but to look at Ma, and I saw that she had tears running down her face as she stood with her back to the kitchen table.

Nothing came to me that I could say to my mother, and Brad was sitting at the table talking about what the Marine recruiter had told him, and how he, Brad, left the ranch early this morning, taking my father's pickup without even telling Dad that he had joined the Marines.

"I left Dad a note saying the pickup would be here, but that I'd be gone, hope that's okay, that I said the pickup would be here at the Home Place," Brad said. "I'd like to see the look on his face when he reads that note, but I'll be long gone, I'll be in Oakland—hell, I might be at Camp Pendleton by then."

I wanted to tell Brad to shut up, but I didn't. I knew Ma didn't want Brad to know she was crying, so I just stood next to her, both of us leaning against the sink, looking out the window, and I put my arm over Ma's shoulder and held us tight together. And then she pulled away a little and dried her hands on her apron; she rubbed her face with her hands and then dried her hands on the apron again.

"It's not a decision I'd have chosen for you, Brad," Ma said. She turned around, walked toward him. "But it isn't for me to choose, is it? I think you've done what you needed to do. I'm just sorry it's what you needed to do."

"Ma, it's okay. It's okay, really." Brad looked at Ma, then got quiet, for a change.

"I can't help thinking about Richard," Ma said.

She was biting her lower lip now, shaking her head after mentioning her brother, who was never talked about after he died in the war.

"You'll never be the same, you'll never be like you are now, and when you come back—" She stopped. "When you come back you will be changed."

The screen door slammed on the side porch.

"Anybody home? I brought the groceries," Gene hollered.

This was Gene's standard line for coming into the house. It was from the "Our Miss Brooks" radio program with Eve Arden. Miss Brooks's delivery boy used it every time he banged into Miss Brooks's house when she was in the middle of a crisis, which was all the time.

"Sorry," Gene said. The big smile on his face faded. "Sorry to interrupt. What are the chances of getting a cup of coffee?"

Ma had already taken a thick white mug from the cupboard and filled it from the Silex percolator on the stove.

"Chances are good," she said. She handed the mug to Gene. "I'm glad you're here, Gene," she said.

"I'd rather say good-bye here, Brad," Ma said. "Would you mind driving Brad down to the post office on Center Street, Gene? Take him to the recruiter's office. Would you mind?"

Gene stood up and took his empty coffee mug to the sink.

"I wouldn't mind at all." He looked at my mother. "We better get the perennials off the back of the pickup, Ace." Gene moved away from the sink, where he had set the coffee mug.

"I think I'll stay here with Ma and Brad."

"I need your help with the plants," Gene said. He motioned with his hand for me to follow. We went outside together.

Gene and I unloaded the pickup and Gene cleaned up the cab a little and then we sat in the cab looking out the windshield, not talking.

Must have been a dozen thoughts pushing their way around in my head then—Ma's words about Brad changing, his never being the same again, wondering what he would be like when he came home. There were thoughts, too, about Uncle Richard and how he died, people in my family not willing to talk about him anymore, not talking about his death, about his never coming home, not alive. I thought about Dad, more than regular thoughts, more like movies in which Dad walked around and talked. I talked back. I was holding Dad, the front of his shirt twisted in my fist, giving him hell, when I realized Gene was talking to me. How long Gene had been talking, I had no idea.

"I guess it's one way to grow up," he said. "But it's a hard way."

"Yeah."

"A guy gets ordered around all the time. Don't think, obey. Up before daybreak. Long marches. Lousy food. Complete loss of yourself as an individual person—that's the worst, that's what would be hardest for me, no individuality. No independence. Always part of the group. No privacy, either. It would drive me crazy."

"Me, too." I was just agreeing. Gene was a bit worked up, and I felt off guard.

"You want to grow up that way?"

"I don't think so."

"There are a lot of romantic notions about Marines, but the truth is they are trained to be a fighting force. They are trained to kill. Not a good way to become a man. That's my thought—not a good way to grow up, to become a man." Gene was quiet then and I didn't say anything, either.

Brad came out of the house alone after a while. He put a small canvas bag in the pickup bed behind the cab. I scooted over next to Gene. Brad sat in the shotgun seat and the three of us squeezed close together while Brad pulled his door shut.

Ma was not on the porch when we left the driveway and I didn't see her through the front windows. I wondered what she said to Brad while they were alone together. Wondered what Brad said. We turned toward Stockton in Gene's pickup.

As we drove along Channel Street close to the waterfront, thick whiffs of tule fog lifted off the water and filled the street. The closer we got to Center Street, the thicker the fog was. The fog rolled in now in dense, swirling mists, blanking out buildings, making it hard to see other cars.

"Damn tule fog," Gene said. He had the pickup lights on.

Neither Brad nor I said anything.

Gene pulled over to the curb across the street from the post office on Center Street and parked. The post office was built like a Greek temple, with six huge marble columns across the front, and above the columns were two nearly naked men carved in marble facing each other in chariots drawn by horses that reared up. But the fog covered the top part of the columns and I couldn't see the men in chariots.

"Guess we're early," Gene said.

The metal grille doors in front of the glass doors of the post office were still chained, locked.

"I'll wait over there in the park," Brad said. He pointed

out his window toward the fountain in the center of Lafayette Park.

"You sure?" Gene said. "I don't mind waiting. Don't mind waiting at all. Do you, Ace?" he said to me.

"No." I shook my head. "I don't mind."

Brad got out his door and reached into the pickup bed for the little canvas bag with handles he had set there. Gene got out of the pickup and came over to the sidewalk.

"I'll wait over there on that bench," Brad said. "Well, thanks, Mr. Tole, thanks for the ride."

Brad began walking backward toward the bench. He looked at us, raised his hand like he was going to wave. Gene and I followed him, facing him. Brad stopped and said, "This is fine. Thanks again. Thanks," he said. He dropped the canvas bag beside him. He held out his hand toward Gene to shake hands.

Gene took Brad's hand like he was going to shake hands, but instead of shaking hands, Gene pulled Brad close and Gene put his arms around Brad and hugged him. I couldn't see Brad's face because of Gene's shoulder; I think this was the first time Brad had been hugged by a man. Gene patted Brad on the shoulders and looked into his face. When Gene moved away he pulled his wallet out of his back pocket and he took a five-dollar bill out of his wallet and gave the bill to Brad.

"Take good care of yourself, young man," Gene said. "And when you come home, I'll buy you a beer."

"I can't take this money," Brad said.

"Yes you can," Gene said. "And someday when you're older, like I am, and you meet a young man who is just getting started, like you are, you'll think, I bet that guy could use a little boost right now, and you can give him five dollars then. That's the way the world works, when it's working right," Gene said.

Brad put the five-dollar bill in his pocket. He held out his hand for me to shake hands, but I put my arms around him like Gene had and I hugged Brad hard, because I didn't know when I'd see him again. I knew that maybe I'd never see him again, knew that was a possibility. I patted Brad on the shoulders, too, like Gene had, and Brad patted me on my shoulders, and then Brad looked at me and said, "Take care of yourself, Ace," called me Ace like Gene called me Ace, and without saying anything more, my brother turned around and walked away.

"Ready?" Gene said. He had the pickup in gear, the clutch held down.

I nodded. We drove off. I watched out the window as Brad walked through the tule fog toward a bench by the fountain in the center of Lafayette Park.

Ceremony

 GENE AND I WERE QUIET AFTER WE
left Center Street, left Brad in Lafayette Park.

I thought about how Brad and I slept together in the
same bed when we were little kids out on the ranch. I
thought about Brad and me riding our bikes through the
walnut orchard, thought about playing Huck and Jim on the
raft in Little John Creek.

An ache came into my chest then, into my stomach,
blocked my throat. I was afraid for Brad, in some way afraid
for myself. But I didn't say anything. Wished life could be
simple again, how it used to be. Life on the ranch, not a perfect life, but life with Dad and Ma, my brother and me
together. A family. Like we cared for each other. Happy. Not
separated, not in danger.

Brad in danger now, alone. Brad's life now daily events I'd never see, never know. Brad meeting people I'd never meet, shooting a rifle, jumping out of an airplane—maybe having sex with a loose woman met in a bar. But I didn't say anything.

Gene drove slow, east through the tule fog. He whistled softly. I could hardly hear. Whistled the song he whistled when he was thinking. We drove east on Webber Avenue past Turner Hardware Store, and the tule fog got wispy again, lifted, disappeared. The sun shone. Gene turned the pickup lights off. He whistled his thoughtful song, the song he said was from *Madama Butterfly*, the story of a Japanese woman who believed her American husband would come back to her one day and she waited. Hopeful.

Gene stopped whistling and said he wanted to go by the Central Valley Nursery to pick something up.

"It'll only take a minute," he said. "I think we can do something nice for your ma. Make your ma feel a little better than she's feeling right now, with Brad gone."

"How?" I said.

"You'll see. Might make you and me feel better, too."

I watched from the pickup as Gene took keys out of his pants pocket and opened the padlock on the wide gates that opened to the road that led into the lath houses that were the main part of the Central Valley Nursery. Gene put his hand back through the laths and stuck the padlock in the hatch without locking it.

Inside the lath house Gene got a hand truck from the

sales area and wheeled the hand truck toward the back of the nursery where the trees were. He turned the corner by the Quonset hut where Vivian Bowers had her office and I couldn't see him anymore.

What I saw next coming back around the Quonset hut was the hand truck with a tree in a ten-gallon can on it. Behind the tree I could see Gene's legs and waist, the top of his body hidden behind the dark green leaves of the tree. He stopped at the office and wrote something on a paper and put the note under a smooth river rock that Vivian used as a paperweight on the sales desk.

Gene wheeled the tree out to the gate and opened the gate again, and I got out of the pickup to help him load the tree.

"It's a dove tree," Gene said. "*Davidia involucrata*. For your ma, for Brad."

Gene unwound a copper wire with a small wood tag on it, took the tag off the tree and handed it to me.

"For your plant log," he said.

I nodded. "*Davidia involucrata*."

Together Gene and I hefted the tree onto the back of the pickup. I got onto the pickup bed and slid the metal can to the front by the cab and gently tilted the tree over flat. Gene got twine out of the cab and tied the limbs close together to protect the leaves from the wind on the ride home. I wedged wooden blocks on each side of the ten-gallon can to keep it from rolling back and forth when Gene turned corners with the pickup.

Gene put the hand truck back in the nursery, picked up a couple of large tree stakes and two tree ties, relocked the gates on his way out, and got in the pickup. Gene and I were quiet again as we drove away from the Central Valley Nursery.

I wondered if Brad was on the bus to Oakland yet, the bus to the Marine Corps. I wondered if Brad had passed through Lathrop, passed over the San Joaquin River on the bridge at the Mossdale Y. Maybe Brad was in Tracy by now. I didn't say anything for a long time.

Then I said, "I wonder where Brad is now."

"Wherever he is, he's on his way," Gene said.

When we got home I went into the house to tell Ma we had a tree to plant and that Gene wanted her to be there when we planted it.

"It's a dove tree," I said to my mother. "*Davidia involucrata*. It's an aristocrat of trees. That's what Gene called it."

Ma reached her hands behind her back to untie her apron. She lifted the loop strap over her head. Ma's eyes were swollen, her nose red, cheeks blotchy. She wiped her hands on the apron before she laid the apron over the back of a kitchen chair.

"I'm going to splash some water on my face," she said. "I'll be right out."

The dove tree sat in the center of the lawn west of the front porch, where the lawn curved in a wide, arching semicircle. Behind the dove tree a distance, off the lawn, were five old valley oak trees and three Monterey pines;

Southern Indica azaleas were planted in masses in the bed around them.

"The perfect place, don't you think, Ace, for a specimen tree like this?" Gene said. "Perfect place."

Gene moved the tree aside and cut a circle in the lawn, pushing his boot down on the top of the shovel blade, rocking the shovel handle back and forth. Gene started digging where he had cut the circle, where the dove tree had been. I got a shovel from the tank house and started digging, too. We put some of the soil from the hole we dug in the wheelbarrow Gene used to move the tree from the pickup. The rest we put in small piles around the hole.

I mixed the soil in the wheelbarrow and in the piles with peat moss from a bag I got in the tank house. Gene cut the ten-gallon can along a seam with a hatchet, using it like a chisel, pounding the hatchet with a hammer. The sides of the can sprang loose from the roots of the tree when Gene got to the bottom of the can seam. He tilted the tree and took the bottom of the can away from the tree roots.

"Pretty neat trick, Gene," Ma said. She stood with a shovel just behind him.

"I've had practice," Gene said. "Put some soil back in the hole, will you, Ace?" he said to me.

Gene lifted the root ball of the tree in his arms and lowered it gently into the hole.

"We want to be careful not to break the soil away from the roots," Gene said. "We want to be sure the crown of the tree—where the root wood and the trunk connect—are at grade, where level ground will be." Gene laid the shovel handle flat over the hole next to the tree trunk to be sure the crown of the tree was at grade.

Then he stood up and brushed his pants and shirt and vest off. He stood beside Ma and me and the three of us looked at the tree sitting unplanted in the hole. Gene brushed his shirt some more and buttoned the buttons of his vest. He left the top button and the bottom button unbuttoned.

"Planting a tree is a significant thing to do," Gene said softly. "It's a sacred thing to do. The right thing to do now, an appropriate way to commemorate Brad's leaving home, Brad's growing up. Planting this tree is a way to mark the event, acknowledge this passage in his life, and in our lives, too." Gene looked at my mother and me.

What my mother was thinking, I don't know, but I was getting a little nervous that Gene might want us to sing a hymn or something.

"Planting a tree seems to me to be the most optimistic thing in the world we can do," Gene said, talking softly, talking to himself. "Planting a tree is not something we do so much for ourselves, for our lifetime. It's a commitment to the future. It's a gift, in a way, that we give to those who will pass by here later, travelers we don't know." He pushed his fists down hard into the pockets of his khaki pants.

"And I guess one thing that can happen"—Gene rocked back and forth a moment on the heels and toes of his work boots—"is that we can care for this tree here in our garden.

We can nurture it. And even though Brad is not here any-more, we can watch the tree grow and we can nourish the tree and hope, imagine, that Brad is healthy and growing, too, nourished wherever he may be."

Gene quit talking. There was a beat of silence. He looked down at his work boot. He moved his boot sideways across the lawn, barely touching the grass, like I had moved my hand across Brad's new haircut.

"That's all. That's all I thought of saying. You want to say something?" he said to Ma, to me.

Ma said, "Thank you, Gene." She looked at him. Tears ran down her cheeks.

"I'll miss Brad a lot," I said. It was just about the stu-pidest, lamest thing I'd ever said. I said it again. "I'll really miss him."

My mother wiped her face on her dress.

"Shall we fill in the dirt, Gene?" she asked.

"Sure," Gene said.

Ma set the shovel she was holding down on the lawn. She dropped onto her knees in front of the hole around the tree. With her bare hands my mother picked up soil and started refilling the empty space around the tree roots.

Gene and I got down on our knees, too, and filled our hands with soil and then emptied the soil into the hole. Gene held the tree trunk steady and looked up into the branches of the young tree to be sure it was planted straight, and left most of the filling of the hole for Ma and me.

"Why don't you get the hose, Ace?" Gene said to me. "We should water the tree in. I'll get the stakes and ties."

After the stakes were driven into the ground with the stake driver and the wire and garden hose tree ties were attached to the stakes and to the trunk of the dove tree just below the first branches, the three of us, Ma, Gene, and I, stood back and silently admired what we had done.

Finally Gene said, "Good work."

"Do all those words help the tree grow?" I asked, thinking of cow pies around the trees on the ranch.

Ma didn't hear me. She said, "Yes," to Gene. "Good work. How about some lunch?" The three of us went into the kitchen together.

After lunch Ma said she was going to lie down for a while. Gene and I went outside to sit on the front steps. Gene took a notepad and pencil out of this vest pocket.

"This is why that tree is called a dove tree," he said, pointing with the pencil. "In the spring, about May, the tree gets flowers on it that only have two petals. They aren't really petals; they're specialized leaves called bracts. The upper bract is about four inches long, the lower, about six." Gene was drawing on the notepad.

"The bracts are rounded and have ruffled edges. You guessed it, Ace." Gene tapped me on the shoulder with the end of the pencil. "They look like doves perched among those vivid green leaves in the spring."

"Sounds neat."

"The true flowers are here in the center." Gene made small crosshatch marks in the center. "Crammed into this little half-inch-wide button. That's what the 'birds and the bees' are after. In the fall the tree has nuts about the size of golf balls"—Gene raised his eyebrows, opened his blue eyes wide—"that hang there on long stems all winter."

That's where we were, Gene and I, sitting on the front porch steps just finishing the drawing of a dove tree flower, when Dad and his hired man, Manuel Podesta, drove up in the Chevy truck.

Gene tore the drawing out of his notebook and handed it to me. We both stood up. I put the drawing in my shirt pocket. Gene and I walked along the brick path to the driveway to meet my father.

Dad
and
the Dove
Tree

 MY FATHER GOT OUT OF THE DRIV-
er's seat. Manuel Podesta, the hired man, moved across the
seat and got behind the steering wheel. Dad slapped the
front fender of the Chevy truck like it was the flank of a
horse, and Manuel backed the flatbed truck around in the
driveway and headed out to the road. He turned east toward
the ranch.

"Where abouts is Brad?" my father said as he approached
Gene Tole and me where we stood at the end of the brick
walkway.

Neither Gene nor I said anything.

"Dad," I said after a bit. "This is Gene Tole. He's
building a garden here for Ma. I'm helping." I sounded like a
third-grader. I hated it, the way I sounded.

"Glad to meet you," Gene said. Gene had his hand out to shake, a wide grin on his face. Gene looked at Dad, watched him.

"Yeah, me too," Dad said. "Lots of work here you've been doing." Gene, Dad, and I were quiet for a moment, then my father said, "Brad in the house?"

"No," I said. "Brad's gone." I felt anxious in my stomach.

"Gone?" my father said. "Gone where?"

"To Oakland," I said. "He's gone this morning to the Marine Corps in Oakland, then to Camp Pendleton or some other camp in South Carolina."

"Ma take him to Oakland?" Dad said.

"No," I said. "Gene and I dropped him downtown, by Lafayette Park. He's on the bus."

Dad looked at me. Looked at Gene. With one hand he took his straw hat off. He ran the fingers of his other hand through his hair, put his straw hat back on.

"Well, shit," Dad said, his voice loud, brittle. "Why would he go off and do that?"

I looked at Dad. When he looked back at me, our gaze stuck for a moment. Dad turned away, looked across the driveway, looked beyond the barn. He didn't look at me for a while after he asked the question.

"Goddammit," Dad said. "How am I supposed to get the goddamned crops harvested without any help?"

He looked at me, expecting me to have the answer. I was quiet while Dad waited for me to answer his question about how to get the crops in without any help.

"Goddammit. Do I have to do everything around here by my fucking self?"

I didn't say anything. I had no answer. I was standing there, I was where he would place his anger. I knew that.

"We planted a tree for Brad this morning, Dad—Ma, Gene, and I," I said. "Want to see it?"

I don't know what I was thinking about. I turned and walked toward the front lawn west of the house. Dad followed. Gene stood aside on the brick walkway as my father passed. Dad took off his straw hat as he walked and wiped his forehead on the sleeve of his blue work shirt.

"This is it," I said. "It's a dove tree." I stood beside the tree. My father stood and looked blankly at the tree. Not understanding.

"It's for Brad, to mark his going away. We can care for the tree here and imagine that Brad is well and healthy wherever he is," I said.

"What a bunch of shit," Dad said. "I won't put up with that kind of crap."

Dad stepped forward and grabbed the tree trunk with one hand. In a single sharp flip, he snapped the head of the dove tree off just above the tree ties. Dropped the head of the tree on the ground in front of me.

I just stood there, my mind gone blank.

There was a hand on my shoulder; Gene gripped my shoulder and pulled me back a short way, put his hand on my chest to move me aside.

Gene knelt down on his haunches, one knee on the

ground, the other raised. He rested his forearm on the raised knee like he was a farmer out in the field thinking, chewing on a stem of wheat in his mouth. He was quiet.

Gene looked up at Dad, spoke softly. "There was no need to do that. Not much is accomplished by destruction."

"Oh, fuck you, Nature Boy."

Dad kicked the branches and leaves of the dove tree that lay on the ground. His boot caught between the branches, branches hanging on to his boot, his leg. Dad kicked his leg in the air several times before the head of the tree shook loose.

"Fuck you." Dad looked right at Gene. Dad's face was red, his eyes didn't stay focused. He turned to me.

"Go pack yourself a bag," he said. "I need help on the ranch. There's real work to do. Not building some fucking flower garden. I've got a crop to get in—real work. Not that you've ever been much help, houseboy."

Hissed, Houseboy, in my face. His face close to mine. His eye twitched, his hands shook.

"Fucking Brad, running out on me. Go get your bag." His hands shook.

Dad pushed me on the chest. I tripped backward, lost balance. One boot caught on the other. I got up quickly.

"This boy is not leaving." Gene's voice, quiet. He stood beside me, hand on my shoulder. "Dave's needed here. He can't go."

"The fuck, you say." Dad's face close to Gene's. "Who are you?"

Dad pushed Gene on the chest like he'd pushed me. Like he'd pushed Brad that day out on the ranch. Dad stepped closer to Gene. Pushed him again. Dad raised his fist, swung at Gene. Gene ducked. Dad's fist flew wild, empty, in the air. He moved after Gene. Swung again.

Gene slipped behind Dad, grabbed him with both arms under Dad's arms. Gene laced his hands together behind Dad's neck. He had my father bent over double. Dad's head held down. His neck bent, chin against chest.

Gene talked quietly to Dad, their heads almost touching.

"Fuck you, Nature—" Dad tried to say. Tried to say "Nature Boy" before Gene tightened his grip. Gene pushed Dad in front of him. They moved toward the tank house, away from me.

Gene walked slightly to one side, talking to Dad.

Then Gene pulled his leg back and kneed my father hard in the butt. Dad's head banged into the side of the tank house.

Gene was still talking to Dad.

He pulled his leg back, kneed my father again, really hard. Dad's head crashed into the wall.

I couldn't think.

Then Ma was standing on the back porch. Watching. Her hand over her mouth, staring at Gene, my father. She ran down the back steps. Stopped at the bottom of the stairs, turned on the water faucet.

"What are you doing?" I was hollering.

"Water. Stops a dogfight." She was calm, her voice determined.

Ma pulled the hose behind her. She held her thumb over the end, made a sharp jet of water. She sprayed cold water on my father. Moved the hose end up and down, a fireman dousing flames. Spray hit Gene, too. Dad held his arms over his face, covered his face as best he could. Water dripped off Gene's hair. His shirt was wet and clung to his body. Ma took her thumb off the hose end and let the cold water run over Dad's head. Dad was soaking wet, water dripping from his hair, his face, off his shoulders, down his pants.

"Get out," Ma said. "Get out. Get out of here and don't come back."

Slowly, gently, Gene let his grip on Dad go. Dad stayed bent over, his shoulder leaning on the side of the tank house, his face pressed against the shingle siding. Dad raised his arm, wiped his face with his wet shirtsleeve.

"Come inside, Gene," Ma said. "You can dry off."

I went in the house, too.

Ma took Gene to the kitchen, then she went into the hall closet to get a towel. I went to the back bathroom and got a bath towel and took it out the back door. Dad was leaning against the tank house upright now. Dazed. I handed him the towel. He held it in his hand but didn't use it. He was breathing hard. Shaking. I took the towel back and wiped his face. Dried his hair. I gave him the towel and he dried his hands and arms.

"Thanks," he said quietly.

I couldn't believe he said it.

I went over to the lawn and picked up his straw hat and gave it to him. Then we walked to his pickup. He didn't say anything more to me. He was still shaking. I opened the door. Dad got into the pickup, sat behind the steering wheel. I closed the door, stood leaning on it, my arm on the window opening.

Dad got keys out of his pocket and started the pickup. He sat there in the pickup looking at me. He turned his head slowly back and forth, not believing, saying no to what had happened, saying, I can't understand this, can't accept it. Tears washed in his eyes, but never made it over the edge. He wasn't able to cry. He lifted his hand from the steering wheel to touch my arm—I think to touch my arm—but was unable to do that, either. Used his hand to hit the steering wheel instead. Moved his head back and forth again.

He pushed the gas pedal a couple times, revved the engine to be sure it was running, backed the pickup around, and drove out the driveway.

I brought the towel back in the house. I could hear Ma and Gene talking in the kitchen. I went outside to the dove tree. It was nothing but a stick in the ground now, standing between two stakes. I put my hand around the stick that had been the dove tree and squeezed.

"It'll grow back," Gene said. He stood beside me. He held a pair of red-handled clippers in his hand. With the clippers he made a new, clean cut diagonally across the tree trunk.

"There is a school of thought," Gene said, "that it's better for a tree to be cut off like this while it's young."

"Sure," I said. "This is great."

"The theory is that the roots grow stronger. Some believe that then the tree puts out more vigorous growth, stronger branches, makes a better tree in the long run. I've never been from that school of thought, though," Gene said, "until now." He laughed. He put his arm over my shoulder. The cool damp of his wet shirtsleeve soaked through my shirt to my skin.

"Guess we didn't get many perennials planted today, did we, Ace?" he said.

"Guess not," I said.

Late that evening I lay on top of the sheets on my bed trying to fall asleep. It was hot outside. Heat from the day's sun was trapped in the wood siding of the house. The heat radiated off the wall, making my bedroom hotter. No breeze was blowing, everything was still.

I thought about what happened that day. These are the pictures I couldn't stop seeing in my mind. My mother spraying Dad with water from the garden hose, running water over him, soaking him. Gene using his knee to hit my father. The dove tree, planting the dove tree, my father breaking it. Brad standing alone in the middle of Lafayette Park, misty tule fog around him, while he waited for the bus to take him to the Marine Corps.

Images came to me from *Red River*, too: John Wayne,

Montgomery Clift, and Joanne Dru getting along just fine, riding off into the sunset, friends again after Joanne Dru shot the gun out of John Wayne's hand and told John Wayne and Montgomery Clift to stop acting like kids.

I wished it was like that in my family. Since Ma hosed Dad down, maybe he would shape up and we could be happy together again.

Lying there on my bed in the hot night air, I remembered the morning my mother and I left the ranch for the last time. I thought about sitting in the front seat of my mother's big old Packard parked in the dark shed, dust motes slicing the dark. What I was thinking of then was the things I would miss. That morning when my mother and I left the ranch she said, "Screw 'em," and we drove away.

Early this afternoon at the Home Place, where Ma was making a new life, building a garden, making the house her own house, she told Dad to leave.

"Get out," she said. "Get out of here and don't come back."

Would I ever see Dad again? I wondered. Ever talk to him like a father and son should talk to each other? Like fathers and sons talked to each other on the radio, on "One Man's Family"? "Father Knows Best"?

I couldn't decide what to do with myself then. Nothing I could do or think made me feel better. There was no place to go. No person to talk to. Except Gene Tole, and he wasn't around. Maybe I could ride my bike over there. I knew where Gene lived, but it was night already. What would I say to

Gene, anyway? Wouldn't have to say anything. Gene would know what to say; he'd ask a question maybe, to make me feel better. Gene could ask a question and make a person feel better, a question like "Can you help it how your father acts?"

"No," I'd have to say, and then I'd feel better. I'd know there wasn't anything I could do to change my father.

I thought about Dad breaking the dove tree again. Gene said the dove tree would grow back better, stronger than before. I didn't see how, but Gene was right about everything else he'd said or done in the garden. But I wondered about this one, about the broken tree.

I remembered Gene's drawing of the dove tree flower that I'd put in my shirt pocket just before Dad drove up. I went to the closet, took my shirt off the peg where I hung my clothes, and got the piece of paper with the drawing of the flower on it.

I sat at my desk by the window, turned on the lamp to look at the drawing. It was simple, just a line that traced the shape of the flower, dots in the center, the part that was the true flower.

I took a bottle of mucilage out of the desk drawer, then opened my plant log to the page where I had written *Davidia involucrata* this morning. The opposite page was empty and I smoothed the paper with the drawing out on it. Looked at it. Thought about how nice it would be to glue Gene's drawing into the book, save it there. Write his name under the drawing, Gene Tole, write the date.

Instead I ripped the paper in two and wadded it up as tight as I could, turning it around and around in my hands, squeezing it with my fingers until it was a tight, hard ball. I threw it across the room. It bounced off the wall and missed the wastepaper basket by the door.

I scooted my chair back and went over to pick up the paper, squeezed it some more, and threw it in the wastebasket.

Made me feel a little better.

One Way to Work It Off

 I WAS SITTING AT THE KITCHEN table eating a bowl of Wheaties, the Breakfast of Champions, when I heard the darnedest noise out back, by the tank house. It startled me. I'd been daydreaming. There I was, tall, handsome, sitting in a canvas chair in front of a tent on the Serengeti Plain, dry grass, hyenas in the distance. A native man wearing feathers and not much else brought me a bowl of millet to eat, banana to slice, and goat's milk to pour on top. I hadn't heard a truck drive up or anything, and when I looked out the window, there was Gene standing at the rear end of a dump truck, the front of the bed high in the air and a huge—I mean really huge—pile of rock sitting on the ground. The truck pulled ahead and more rock slid out the back of the bed. Then the driver let the dump bed down with a bang. He came around behind the truck with a clip-board and handed it to Gene. The driver took his baseball cap off his head and used it to slap his thigh a couple times, dust flying where he slapped. Gene signed a paper on the clipboard and handed it back. He waved and the driver got in the cab and drove off.

The screen door slammed and Gene came into the kitchen.

"Coffee, anyone?" he said.

"Pot's on the stove, help yourself," I said.

"We have some rock out there, Ace, potential wall."

"I heard it. Saw it, too. Potential work if you ask me."

I upended my cereal bowl and drank what was left of the milk. Ma was still in the bathtub; hard for her to correct my manners from there. Gene sat down with a mug of coffee in his hand and leaned back in the chair.

"Going to be a scorcher out there today. Sooner we get started, the better." Gene stood up and carried his coffee mug out the back door. I put my cereal bowl in the sink and followed.

I stood on the back porch a moment and stretched in the sun. The early-morning air felt dense, heavy with moisture, damp on my skin. Everything was still. The only sound, birds chirping and calling. Sunlight was bright, freshly scattered across the land. Soon the sun would pull the dew off the grass, lift the moisture from the soil, and change the damp into air, but for now the morning was full of thickness and a sense of sleep and of the world coming slowly to life.

I walked down the steps, looked up at the sky: bright blue above, fading to white at the horizon as far as I could see. I stretched some more.

Gene stood leaning over the front fender of his pickup, the plan he had drawn for the garden spread out on the pickup hood in front of him.

"This day is going to be a doozie. Better get started before we get toasted out of business. Come have a look." He smoothed creases out of the plan with the side of his hand.

I stood beside Gene, leaning against the fender, elbows propped on the hood. The scent of aftershave was sweet and musky at the same time, like wildflowers, Gene's smell, not a smell I'd noticed on other men.

The plan showed a perennial garden in the mostly flat area between the house, the tank house, and the barn, where my mother parked her car.

Gene picked up the plan and looked toward the tank house.

"The problem is that back here." He walked to the rear of the tank house, not finishing his thought, and pointed across the open space to the barn.

"Back here, the grade slopes down toward the pit. We want the beds to be level, so we build a low retaining wall across here, adds an architectural element."

"What would we do without an architectural element?" I said.

Gene turned and looked at me, pretending to be hurt.

"We'd be lost without an architectural element," I said.

"This is serious." He laughed.

Gene was talking fast then, waving his arms and pointing like a policeman directing traffic.

"The terrace is raised just a step or two and it becomes a sitting area, a place where people gather and talk and look out over the sunken garden, not the pit anymore, but not too grandiose."

He traced a line across the plan with his finger. "The retaining wall is the first step. The wall, the terrace, and the perennial beds tie the buildings together, enclose the space. Make any sense?"

"Sure," I said.

When Gene finished talking, the first thing we did was stretch a chalk line from the tank house to the barn.

"Take the shovel and level a strip of ground about this wide right under the line." Gene held his hands out about two feet apart. He attached a level to the chalk line and ran the level along the line to be sure the wall base was flat.

"Can't put it off any longer," Gene said. "It's rock-moving time." He walked to the rock pile and picked up a rock slab and held it against his waist. He walked, carrying the rock, to the leveled place by the tank house and set the rock on the ground. He moved the rock around until it rested solid. I did the same. Back and forth we went like a couple of worker ants.

The lifting and carrying took a lot of breath and we didn't say much to each other. Building the wall was important work, made me feel like a real craftsman. Gene called what we were doing dry-wall construction, and I was thinking about all the people in the world who had built walls and houses and other things with stone. I was going through my list of stone projects, dreaming about work on the Pyramids, the Great Wall, the Parthenon, and the Roman Forum, when Gene announced it was ten o'clock.

"Time for a break," he said.

I went into the house to get us a couple glasses of iced tea. When I got back outside with the iced tea, Gene was sitting on top of the rocks that were the beginning of the wall, wiping his face with a bandanna. I handed him a glass and sat beside him. We drank our iced tea without talking much, then for no reason Gene had to pull Dad out of the blue and start talking about him.

"Heard from your dad since . . . that incident the other day?" he asked.

"We won't hear from him," I said.

"I thought he might call. Might apologize. Something like that." Gene bent forward, rested his forearms on his knees, held the glass of iced tea between his hands.

"Dad? You don't know Dad very well."

"I don't. I just thought—hoped—maybe he'd get in touch. Make amends. He was pretty angry when he was here, wasn't he?"

"He gets that way sometimes."

"I guess it was Brad leaving that he was upset about. Get-

ting the harvest done. You think so? Or was it really something else?"

"I don't know," I said. "I can't tell. You can never tell
with Dad. What might make him mad." I reached down and
picked a small smooth stone from the dust. Tossed the stone
back and forth between my hands. "Sure took it out on the
dove tree, though, didn't he? Darn it, he wrecked the dove
tree. Really made me mad."

I was scuffing my boots in the dust, kicking dirt.

"What do you do when you get that way?" Gene was
looking at me closely, I could tell. "When you're mad, what
do you do? You break things up, too?"

"I don't know. I just get mad. Stay mad, I guess. I guess
that's what I do."

I bent over and picked up more small rocks, loose gravel.
I stood up and threw them one at a time out into the open
air above the pit and watched as they hit the ground in the
distance.

Gene stood up, too, and bent to gather a handful of
rocks. He placed his feet far apart, one in front of the other,
and hauled off with a powerful throw putting a rock so far
out over the pit I lost sight of it until it landed in a quick
puff of dust. He picked another rock from his handful and
threw it. We didn't talk, both throwing rocks. I was trying to
keep up with him, to see if I could outdistance him, but I
couldn't. We kept throwing rocks, fast and furious, and suddenly Gene started to laugh.

"What's so funny?" I said.

"The two of us," he said, "standing here throwing rocks like a couple kids."

"I am a kid."

"Not quite a kid, Ace."

"You don't think so?"

"A young man, I'm afraid."

I stopped throwing rocks and looked at Gene, pleasure going off inside me, made me warm, my skin prickly all over at what he'd said.

"We can act like kids for a while," I said.

"You bet we can." Gene bent over, gathering rocks. "Here, have a few more." He poured rocks from the palm of his hand into mine, our hands touching.

"This is one way to work it off," he said.

"Work what off?"

"Anger."

"Oh, that."

"Yeah, that. What did you think?"

"I don't know."

We stood looking at the pit, looking at each other once in a while, our talk stalled, not having anything to say, not knowing what to say. Then I was blurting, not thinking, just blurting things out.

"I'm sorry Dad called you Nature Boy. I don't know why he said that, why he said 'Fuck you' to you. I don't know why."

"Christ, it's not your fault. It didn't bother me much, anyway. I've been called worse."

"You been called worse? When? Who would?"

Gene laughed, slapped me on the shoulder, said, "Let's not go into that, Ace."

I laughed a little. "He had no business saying those things, no business being that way, the way he is sometimes."

"You're not responsible for your dad, how he behaves."

"He didn't make me feel very good. I didn't feel very proud the other day, I can tell you that."

"You treated him well, though. I saw you out the kitchen window, watched you go get his hat, bring him a towel, help him dry off. You treated him pretty damn well, I'd say. Maybe you can't be all that proud of him, but you can be proud of yourself, how you behaved. More important, I'd say, to be proud of how you behaved. Your dad can take care of himself."

Gene and I were quiet for a while then. I looked over across the yard at the dove tree, nothing but a stick now between two stakes. I turned back; Gene was watching me.

"You really think it'll grow back?"

"I'm sure it will. Give it a couple months."

"It was such a pretty tree."

"It'll be pretty again. Listen, you know what? This wall isn't going to build itself, Ace, not with us just sitting on it. Why don't you throw a few rocks from that pile at it?" He tossed a small rock at the pile of stones for the wall.

"Suppose so," I said.

"Try and hold your enthusiasm down." Gene put his hand on my straw hat and pushed it low over my ears.

I pulled my hat up from where it was stuck on my forehead and walked to the rock pile.

"See one there that fits into this slot?" Gene put his hand on a notch in the wall between two large flat rocks.

I moved a rock off the pile, sliding it down onto the ground. I moved a few more rocks and found a square-shaped one that looked about the right size. I picked it up and carried it partway to the wall and heaved it toward Gene, using my body strength to throw it. The rock hit the ground and rolled close to the wall.

"Perfect," Gene said.

I was back at the rock pile rooting around for a better-shaped rock. Found it. "How about this one?" I threw it over toward the wall. That's how I got started moving the rock pile from where it was dumped to the wall. I started moving the pile, rock by rock, then got the wheelbarrow, moving several rocks at a time. I was running, then pushing the wheelbarrow before me, dumping the barrow, racing back for more.

Gene was setting the rock in the wall. He had his shirt off and worked in a white undershirt without sleeves, just straps over his shoulders. Dark hair grew across his chest, showed above the white T-shirt.

•　•　•

Later in the afternoon, I sat on the stone wall beside Gene and we drank fresh iced tea slowly and looked across the pit where my great-grandfather had dug clay for the brickyard and my mother had decided not to build a sunken garden because it would be too grandiose.

Gene started to get up from the wall. He pushed his hands down on his knees and reared his butt off the stones, acting like an old man who has done too much hard work that day. He put his hand on my shoulder for support and gave my shoulder a push.

I lost balance on the stone wall and rolled backward, iced tea flying, my legs and feet shooting into the air, trying to recover from the force of Gene's push. I tumbled over backward and landed in the dirt on the other side, my feet in the air, soles of my shoes facing up, what Dad called ass-over-teakettle.

Gene looked over the wall at me. "I didn't mean to sink you like that." He said *sink* in a funny way, like I was the *Titanic* and he was the iceberg.

I didn't answer. I was lying on my back, feet in the air, laughing. Gene jumped up on the wall and grabbed my ankles in his hands and pulled me up. He held me hanging upside down that way, then swung me to the side, dropped my leg and grabbed my hand and with one quick flip stood me upright again.

"You should be more careful," he said. "You can't trust a stone wall."

"Sure," I said. I was laughing and brushing my butt and back off. "Like the problem is with the wall."

We went back to work, sun shining overhead, working its way west. Gene and I both wore wide-brimmed straw hats.

"You remind me of how I was when I was your age," Gene said. "That's why I like working with you, Ace, why I like doing things together, being friends."

I kept moving for a while, but my mind was stopped, stopped on "I like working with you, I like doing things together, being friends." Then I stopped moving, too, stood leaning against the wheelbarrow. The best feeling came into me then from Gene saying he liked being friends, like being together because I reminded him of when he was young, when he was my age.

Maybe it was the sun. Maybe it was the need to stop lifting and setting rock in the afternoon heat. Maybe it was just the need to talk. Whatever it was, Gene Tole stopped working on the rock wall, stood up, stretched, took off his straw hat, and wiped his forehead and neck with the red bandanna he had in his back pocket.

"So, what do you think?" I said.

"What do I think about what?" Gene said.

"Subject of your choice," I said. I just wanted him to talk.

Gene walked to the tank house and sat down in the shade, rested his back against the wall, tilted his head back. He looked up into the white sky. He wiped his face, a red crease around his forehead where his hat rested, his hair wet, flattened on the sides, poufed up on top. Hat hair, he called it.

"Oh, I don't know," he said. "Why don't you get us another glass of iced tea, Ace."

When I got back outside with two glasses and the pitcher of iced tea my mother had made, Gene Tole had moved under the oak tree. His legs stretched before him, back against the rough bark of the tree trunk. I sat down beside him, legs out front resting, too, like Gene. Gene smoothed a spot in the dust and drew pictures with a twig. Nothing I could make out, though.

The Most
Natural
Thing
in the World

 "TIME TO CALL IT A DAY," GENE
said.

"You're telling me!" I said.

"How about a dip in the irrigation ditch down Pock Lane? Ask your ma if you can go for a swim."

I went into the house and told Ma Gene Tole and I were going swimming.

"How nice. You've earned it, moving all that rock. Be back by supper time," she said. "Meatloaf."

I took two towels from the bathroom closet and got my swimming trunks with palm trees and hula girls on them from my bedroom dresser upstairs.

Gene drove the Studebaker along Pock Lane past Matsuda's place, open fields on both sides, vast spreading farmland, once in a while a house. Heat waves shimmering up from the road ahead of us, pale blue sky dome overhead, fading to white at the horizon. The air still, hotter than the gates of hell, in Ma's words. We crossed the irrigation canal on a small concrete bridge and turned onto a dirt road that followed along beside the canal.

What little breeze the pickup stirred felt good on my arm, elbow out the window. Across the field three Mexican laborers moved syphon pipes over rows of tomato plants. Gene stopped near a big willow tree growing beside the canal.

The pickup had barely quit rolling before Gene threw open the door. He slid out of his seat and stood on the dusty road beside the truck, pulling his undershirt over his head like the shirt had caught on fire. He untied his shoelaces, tossed his shoes in the back of the pickup, pealed off his socks, each in a single movement, tossed them on top of the shoes. He practically ran barefoot up the canal bank, wading through a mass of dark green mint plants. From the pickup, I watched Gene as he stood on one foot at the top of the levee. He pulled his khaki shorts off one leg, then the other, a natural balancing act.

I climbed out of the pickup, leaving the towels and my trunks, and walked up the path Gene had trampled in the spearmint. Crushed mint fragrance ran through the air, made the place smell scrubbed and crispy clean. The only sound came from bees working the dense, purple clusters of mint flowers. I slipped my T-shirt off as I walked through the plants, mint leaves scratching my legs, the scent of mint around me, on me.

Gene stood naked with his back to me, sun reflecting on his blond hair, lighting it the color of gold and copper. He turned to me. I was startled, looked at my shoes and began taking them off.

"Better hurry," he said. "Never can tell when somebody in Sacramento will flip a switch and dry this up."

I looked at him again as he turned his back. He stood a moment in the sun, then strolled down the canal bank to the water.

Gene was as comfortable with his clothes off as he was with them on. He looked like being at the irrigation canal with no clothes on was the most natural thing in the world to him. He looked like he didn't care who saw him, didn't care what they thought if they did.

Gene was right in his comfort, it fit him. But I didn't understand how he was so right in his comfort and being naked was wrong for me. That's what I felt, though, seeing him naked like that, afraid myself to be naked. All at the same time, right and wrong both, a paradox.

A big splash shot from the irrigation canal and Gene was gliding underwater, head and chest almost touching the sandy canal bottom. Then he stood up on the other side of the irrigation canal, feet on the sandy bottom, water swirling around his legs.

Horsetail rush grew along the bank and plants that looked like tiny four-leaf clovers floated on the water's surface. The current pulled the floating clover leafs on the wire-thin stems that anchored them to the bottom. Water dripped from Gene's hair, ran across his face and down his chest, between his legs.

"Come on in, Ace," he hollered.

I stood on the levee in my white Jockey shorts, then walked down the bank into the water. The water was clear and cold, running fast, the current strong. It pushed around my ankles, up my calves, and covered my thighs. The water made my skin feel like it was early morning, my skin just waking up.

I stood still in the water, my toes curled in the soft loam. I moved in deeper. Water soaked my Jockey shorts, my shorts tight and clingy around my waist, showing everything I had, dick, balls, the works. Why didn't I have enough sense to wear my swimming trunks, hula girls on them? I turned my back, bent down, and stripped my Jockey shorts off, tossed them up on the bank. I stood there, my hands in front of me for a while, until I felt more ridiculous like that than I would with myself exposed, and then I flopped facedown in the water.

I swam across the irrigation ditch. Gene ran up the bank and stood on the top of the levee, brushing water off his arms and chest. He dashed along the levee a short ways and grabbed a rope that dangled from a willow branch. He pulled the rope way back, leaning his weight against it. He grinned at me, then ran across the top of the levee, jumping in the air at the last second, swinging from the rope in a wide arc, coasting through the blue above the water. His dick swinging between his legs, balls hanging tight behind it. Gene's legs were in front of him, a circus performer on the trapeze. Before he let go, he arched his back, his legs and feet up in the air, hair hanging, shining. Dick hanging, shining, too. Then he let the rope go. Sheets of water sprayed around me when Gene hit.

I ran up the bank and caught the rope, still swinging, and pulled it back, then raced as fast as I could across the levee, then no levee, my feet still running out in the open, touching nothing, nothing under them but water, and that way below, far enough below to be scary, be thrilling.

The rope reached the end of its arc, as far out over the canal as my weight carried it, and I let my hands go, dropping for the longest time, dropping in slow motion, until my feet hit the water, the crack sound of their breaking the surface, just enough time to grab my nose and not get a snout full of water, and then the plunge of water, bubbles rushing up all over me.

We took turns on the rope, Gene and I, and we laughed and talked about how good we were at swinging on the rope, saying, "Hey, watch this." Gene tried to show me how to push at the end to make my feet go in the air and drop head-first into the water the way he did. But I couldn't do it, turned into belly flops every time.

"You're heavier, you swing further out," I said.

"Tell you what, you swing out over the ditch and don't let go. Swing back in."

I took the rope, ran out, sailed over the water and swung back toward the land, watching it, lifting my knees when I came toward the levee. Gene was running as fast as he could across the levee toward me; I was still moving toward him over the levee top.

"Hold on," he hollered.

Just as I started to swing back over the water, Gene made a powerful lunge toward me and grabbed the rope, his hands gripping just above mine. With the force of his weight and his momentum we sailed out into the open above the water, our bodies pressed together, Gene's arms around my head, my head against his chest. I closed my eyes.

"Now," he called out. He grasped my hands and pulled them from the rope. We were suspended, and then falling together like that, and we hit the water, Gene still holding my hands clasped together in his. And then he let go, the two of us going deeper under the water, and I opened my eyes and he was close, looking at me, his eyes open, too. He was smiling, bubbles escaping his lips, he was laughing.

When we got out of the water and stood a moment on the top of the levee, Gene said, "Let's rest a bit. Water's pretty cold."

We sat down on the grass in the sun, each of us hugging our knees.

Gene brushed water from his shoulders and ran his fingers through his hair, combing it straight back away from his face and eyes. We watched the water flow by. I pulled a grass stem and had it in my mouth chewing it. Gene leaned all the way back in the grass and stretched his legs before him, closed his eyes. I watched the water and watched Gene, thought what a handsome man he was, how well built, wished I'd be so well built someday, when I grew up. And I laid back like Gene was, hands under my head, and put my legs out in front of me, too, and continued chewing on my piece of grass, and then I heard Gene's heavy breathing, breathing in and out, regular, soft, and I knew he had fallen asleep, and I was lying right there in the open, nothing around anywhere but sun and grass, water running by, and the willow tree and Gene's shoulder only a couple inches from mine, and I wished that I could reach over and touch him, caress him with just my fingertips, but I couldn't.

I had such strong longing feelings for him right then, they caught in my throat. I had to sit up. Coughed.

"Damn grass," I said quietly. Threw the grass away.

Gene's breathing still the same, regular. Sleeping.

I lay back down on my side, head propped on my hand, looking at Gene. Sun hitting my shoulders, my back feeling hot, maybe getting sunburned.

Gene turned his head suddenly, looking at me. Maybe he sensed I was watching him. He was breathing fast, not like when he was sleeping. He sat up and held his knees again.

After a moment he said, "We better get going."

"Think so?" I said.

"Your ma will wonder what the hell happened to you. She'll figure you drowned in the irrigation ditch."

"I doubt it," I said.

But Gene was already standing up. He walked across the levee toward the pickup. He bent down, gathering his clothes as he walked, putting on his underwear, then his shorts. I got up and followed. He was sitting in the pickup ready to go when I got there.

Gene turned the Studebaker around and we headed toward Pock Lane, dust flying from the tires, hanging in the still air, drifting only slightly. We turned onto the paved road and headed toward home. Gene looked out his window at the alfalfa field, didn't say anything, neither did I.

We rode along like that looking out our windows. I let my arm catch the breeze.

"You know, Ace," Gene said, "you take stuff pretty seriously."

I couldn't think of what to say. Taking stuff pretty seriously sounded like a fault. I didn't say anything, just looked at Gene, the outline of his face framed in the door window, bright sunlight behind him, his arm propped against the top of the door, thumb gripped inside.

"You know something, Ace? You really do remind me of myself, when I was your age." His voice soft. "I was a serious young man, too."

"You were?" I breathed in, held it, watched a flock of red-winged blackbirds on the fence beside the road ahead.

"Sure was." Silence again. The pickup approached the blackbirds. They broke into flight.

"It's good to work with you, Ace, doing things together, being friends."

Best friends, I thought, friends who stick together, always. That's what Gene meant, not exactly what he said, but what he meant.

Gene looked at me, we watched each other. "Makes me feel like I can help a bit. Help you understand the way things are."

Out the window the birds soared into the blue-white sky, banked, changing direction, vanished, turned again, wheeling into sight.

I was watching the birds, but my mind stopped on "I like working with you, Ace, like doing things together, being friends." Excitement like the bird's flight inside me, Gene saying what he said, liked being friends, being together.

I could grow up to be like Gene Tole.

Late-afternoon light was behind Gene. He looked forward again, his features in shadow, his face a line.

"It's not easy," Gene said. "Nobody said it would be easy, and for a damn good reason—it isn't easy."

"I guess."

Gene shifted the pickup into neutral and we coasted to a stop at Mariposa Road. Gene looked right and left, his blond hair curling up at the back of his neck and over his ears from being wet. I looked right and left, too.

Gene was telling me about life and that things could get rough, but that a person has to keep trying.

"You'll figure it out," he said.

I was taking it in, all the things Gene was saying, feeling that everything was going to be all right after all—starting a new school, it was going to be okay—and then there it was: my father's blue Chevy truck rolling along the road right in front of us.

I couldn't see my father driving. Saw a white straw hat like my father wears in summertime. Saw his arm move fast out the window, raised above the cab, his hand waving. Could be Manuel Podesta, maybe, my father's hired man. But I knew the wave, recognized the striped blue work shirt. Tractor tire behind the cab, my father, sure enough, headed back to the ranch after picking up a new tire at Farmer's Equipment.

Gene was still talking when the truck passed. He let the clutch out and we drove the short distance up the road, Gene talking the whole time, telling me how to live life, what was important, what wasn't.

"Was that your dad's truck we saw down at Pock Lane?" he asked.

"I think so."

"I do, too. Too bad he didn't stop. We could have gone down to the Little Store and all had us a Coke." Gene steered the pickup into the driveway at the Home Place, talking, saying he would see me tomorrow, more rock wall tomorrow, he was saying.

I said thanks to Gene for taking me swimming. I said I liked working together, too. Doing things together. Said I was glad he was my friend. Said it felt good to me to be friends, too. Said, See you in the morning.

I went into the house then. Said hi to my mom. She said supper was almost ready, wash up for supper. Meatloaf, she said. Okay, I said, and I went up the back stairs to my bedroom, and I looked out the window at the perennial garden Gene and I were building, the evening still filled with light, and I wondered how I could tell Gene Tole I wished he was my father, not my father. And what kind of son was I that I wanted another man to be my father when I already had a father.

"It's not easy," I said. "Nobody said it would be easy—for a damned good reason."

Things About
Me
You Don't
Know

 THE FIRST TIME I HEARD A SYM-
phony orchestra, it started like this. In the morning Ma came
outside in slacks and a white cotton blouse. She had her hair
up in curlers and wrapped in a bandanna tied in a knot in
front. She went to the garage where she parked her car and
she backed her car out and left it there on the gravel driveway. Ma went back in the house and came out with a bucket.
Soapsuds sloshed over the top of the bucket as she walked.

"Want to help wash the car?" she said, her voice all
bouncy and full of enthusiasm, like washing the car was
going to be the sports event of the year.

"Sure," I said, "I'll help."

I went to my room and changed into cutoffs and a
T-shirt. I put my tennis shoes on without socks. When I got

235

outside Ma had rinsed the car with the hose to get it wet. She was bent over the front, washing the grille of the old Packard with a sponge.

"You take that side," she said, "and I'll do this one. Don't leave any spots. They don't show when the car is wet, but they're awful when it dries."

"I won't," I said.

I just finished my side of the hood and was on the front fender when Ma said, "I got us tickets to the symphony tonight."

"Oh," I said.

"I thought it would be good for you. You've never seen anything like the symphony, never heard anything like it. It won't hurt you to broaden your horizons."

"I didn't know there was anything wrong with my horizons."

I put the sponge in the bucket and went to turn on the faucet to hose down the hood and the front fender on my side of the car.

"My horizons feel just fine," I said.

"Don't be such a freshie. You know what I mean. The symphony will be a good experience for you."

I was washing the door on my side of the car.

"I got you a new pair of black pants to wear," Ma said.

I straightened up and looked through the car window. Across the front seat I could see my mother looking at me through the window on her side.

"Black pants?" I said.

"I ironed your white shirt—it'll still fit just fine. You can wear your light gray sweater. I bought you a new necktie, too. You'll look perfect."

"What is this, church? A funeral?"

"Not exactly. It's not a funeral, not church, but you're close. It's a requiem mass. I understand it's lovely."

"Great."

"It's a rare opportunity. A friend gave us the tickets."

Ma looked through the car at me, her face bunched up, showed her awkward feeling.

"I don't really want to go alone," she said. "I think it'll be fun. I bought myself a new dress, too. It'll be fun. You might see someone you know there."

Ma went inside and I was left with a chamois, flipping it out over the car, dragging it back across the hood to make sure there were no streaks. Wringing the chamois out, feeling kind of funny about going to the symphony, lost in thought.

I actually jumped when Parkie said, "What you doing that for?" right behind me.

"Give you three guesses," I said. "First two don't count."

"Those come off dead goats. You know that, don't you? That's a dead goat's skin you got there in your hands." He pointed.

I just looked at him awhile. "You expect me to use a live one?"

I held the chamois over Parkie's shoes and wrung it out. He shuffled backward.

"What you doing tonight? You want to see if we can do something together? I'm sick of baby-sitting my mother. I can't stand my sister, she's a bitch. What a bitch. Maybe we can do something. What you say?"

"I can't, Parkie. I'm going out."

"Where you going?"

I didn't answer. Kept drying the car.

"Where to?" he asked.

"To the symphony."

"The what?"

"You heard," I said.

"Sure I heard, but I can't believe. Why?" He was leaning on the other side of the hood, his T-shirt soaking up water where I hadn't yet dried.

"It's a rare opportunity." I tried to sound like Ma.

" 'Rare opportunity.' Like not cooked all the way through? Bloody in the middle? I believe that part all right." He was laughing, his flesh shaking around on the hood.

"My mother has it all planned."

"And I thought I had it rough."

He straightened up and walked around the car, his hands behind his back, trying to look like Napoleon at Waterloo.

"Listen, you need company on this one. Tell you what. I'll keep you company. I got to get out of the house. I'm going crazy. They're driving me crazy. What is a symphony exactly, anyway? I know it's awful, but what is it?"

"Tonight it's a symphony orchestra playing a requiem mass, I guess. That's what Ma says, that's all I know."

"Oh Jesus, I take my offer back. That's way too much, uh-uh. You're my friend, I'd like to help you out, but uh-uh, that's just too much."

"I don't have another ticket anyway, Parkie."

"You mean you're paying for this? Oh God. Listen, I'll see you later," he said. "This is too much. Way too much."

Without saying good-bye, Parkie walked off, still doing his version of Napoleon, like he was without a friend in the world, and I felt sorry for him, just like he wanted me to feel sorry for him.

But I wished I could do something to cheer him up, help him get out of his house. He was a friend after all.

Ma and I sat in seats in the second row of the balcony of the Civic Auditorium in Stockton. There was one other time I had been in the Civic Auditorium and that was to see the Shriners' Circus. I could tell this was going to be nothing like the Shriners' Circus. A short, stout, older woman with blue hair and a couple of dead foxes over her shoulders sat in the row in front of us, a fox head on each shoulder, bright glass eyes eyeing everyone around the lady, and paws holding on to her bulging back and huge breasts.

The program said this was the San Francisco Symphony Orchestra's summer season and the orchestra was on tour to bring fine music to rural areas.

I read on in the program to see what was in store.

"Who wrote this?" I asked Ma. "I can't even pronounce the guy's name."

"Giuseppe Verdi. Give it a chance."

"Couldn't they get a guy with a decent-sounding name, something a person could say?"

"He was Italian," Ma said. "Joe Green. Call him Joe Green if it makes you feel better."

The people in the orchestra were finding seats in a big semicircle around a box on the floor with a step on one side. They were dressed in black and white, the women in long dresses, the men with ruffled shirts. Some people in the orchestra were already seated, making noise with their instruments. Joe Green music.

More men and women dressed in white shirts and blouses, black pants and skirts, started filing onto bleachers set up around the orchestra.

"That's the chorus." Ma pointed. "People from local church choirs and from the College of the Pacific."

It took a long time for the chorus to get onto the risers. The men and women in the chorus carried folders of music and chattered to one another like excited birds. The women held their long skirts away from their shoes as they climbed to their places. It was one big deal, I could tell that much. The noise of excited people talking got louder.

I watched the chorus closely as they climbed onto the bleachers. I figured one or two of them would trip, for sure, and knock half a dozen others over like dominos. That's how I happened to spot Gene Tole.

"Hey, there's Gene down there." I pointed so Ma could see him.

"I knew he would be. He gave us the tickets."

"I'll be damned," I said.

"You'll be quiet," Ma said. "This is no place for talk like that."

Gene steadied the woman in front of him, holding on to her elbow as she climbed the risers. When she was settled Gene found his place in the row behind her and grinned at the man standing next to him, whispered something. The guy laughed, looked at Gene and nodded.

The conductor came out, stood on his platform, took a bow. The crowd was wild with clapping. Two women and two men all dressed up came out and sat down in chairs in front of the orchestra, facing the audience.

The lights in the Civic Auditorium dimmed and the conductor pointed to the people in the chorus and raised his hands. The chorus members lifted their music as if one string pulled all their arms together, Gene's arm among them. The conductor had a baton in one hand, held it high a moment, then brought his arms down sharply and we were off.

The music came out strong and sweet, made my skin bumpy. I was warm and excited. Watched Gene.

At one point the voices in the choir made a sound that spiraled through the air, like falling. Sounded dizzy.

Ma leaned over. "Souls are being pushed out of purgatory and dropping to hell," she whispered in my ear.

The sound of souls screaming on their way to hell was my favorite part. I guess Verdi liked it, too, he managed to write it in again later on.

It was after the lights came back up and people finally stopped clapping and started milling around, walking toward the door to the hall and stairway outside the balcony, that Ma met one of her garden club friends. Ma introduced me to her friend, Emmie Lingren, and Emmie introduced her brother George to my mother and me. Emmie, Ma, and George Anderson started talking, ignored me.

"I'm going to see if I can catch up with Gene, Ma."

"Fine, dear," Ma said.

What's this "dear" stuff, ran through my mind, sarcastic. Ma never called me dear. Not a good time to start now.

"I'll meet you by the columns out front in a few minutes," she said.

Downstairs, I fought my way through the crowd coming from the seats on the first floor. Orchestra members were packing up their instruments and talking to one another like this was just another day's work. People in the choir were coming down off the risers. Gene walked slowly, hardly moving along the riser, then waited for the people in front of him to move. He saw me, waved back, grinned. Then he turned his head toward the man behind him and said something. Gene laughed, looked at me again and raised his eyebrows, rolled his eyes in a way that said, Will these people ever get moving?

I stood waiting at the bottom of the risers. Gene put his hands on the shoulders of the man in front of him and pulled the man back until the man's shoulders rested against Gene's chest. Gene spoke into the man's ear. The man shook his head, meant no, then shrugged his shoulders. He looked at Gene, smiled and said something, and Gene patted the man's shoulder.

When Gene reached the floor, he was still talking with three of his choir friends. They moved as a group away from where I waited. I walked after them. When I got closer, I realized from what I heard that Gene and his friends were planning to go out somewhere. I stood beside Gene, waited a bit before he noticed me.

I looked around to see if anyone was watching. What would they think? I shifted back and forth, one foot, the other, my fists pushed into my pants pockets.

He turned to me, his music tucked under his arm. "Did you like it?"

"Pretty nifty," I said. "The part where the souls are going to hell, that was great."

Gene's men friends stood around talking to one another, paying no attention to us.

"Naturally, you'd like the souls going to hell." Gene laughed.

Gene and I were quiet standing there together. He was listening to what his friends were saying.

Suddenly, I knew I didn't fit in, didn't know how to. I

didn't belong here. In over my head with these people, this was no place for me. I couldn't stay, no way to leave without looking stupid?

"I had no idea you could sing," I said. Hoped it would help if I talked.

"It ever occur to you that there might be lots of things about me you don't know?" We stood close together, Gene looking directly at me. "Ever think about that?" He kept staring at me. I had to look away.

"I guess I hadn't thought about it." I wished to hell I was somewhere else. Didn't know what to do or say, people standing around Gene and me, friends of his from the choir, and me getting set straight about Gene's life, being told I didn't know that much about him.

The men Gene was with from the choir started walking slowly to the back of the auditorium.

"I'm sorry," I said. "I never thought much about what you did when we weren't together." A sad feeling came over me. I guess it showed.

"Don't take it so hard," Gene said. "My life is pretty boring. Nothing too exciting, a little singing now and then." He laughed and put his hand on my shoulder, squeezed my shoulder, shook me gently.

"Hey, Tole. You coming or not?" It was the guy who'd stood beside Gene in the choir.

Gene gave my shoulder a pat, took his hand away. "Be right there," he said. "Take it easy, Ace. Thanks for coming."

He turned around, walked fast to catch up with his friends, and they all went out the back door of the Civic Auditorium together, arms slung around one another.

I turned around, standing in the empty cavern of the Civic Auditorium alone except for a few orchestra people putting music in their cases, tucking their instruments away until the next performance, maybe practice, maybe a concert in Fresno, maybe Bakersfield. No one here I knew, the balconies empty now, the place where Ma and I had sat empty, a single usher walking along rows of seats, tilting empty seats up where people forgot to do it when they left.

I found Ma waiting out front, put my arm out for her to take, and she put her hand over my arm like she was my date.

"The music was great." I looked over at Ma when I said it.

"You liked it? I was afraid you wouldn't."

"I loved it, Ma." We walked awhile without talking. "It was a surprise to see Gene, though," I said. "I had no idea he sang. I wonder why he never mentioned it to me. Working together all this time, and he never said anything about singing."

"I was so glad to meet George Anderson," Ma said.

She didn't say anything about what I'd just said about Gene, didn't leave room for me to tell her about Gene going off with his friends from the choir.

"Emmie has been telling me about him. He asked me to go out to dinner with him next Saturday. I'm excited."

"Great, Ma," I said. It didn't take a second for half a dozen questions about my mother and George Anderson to get into my head and start circling around in there.

"It's just dinner," she said. "Here, why don't you drive home. I'm all nerves." She handed me the keys to her car.

"I don't have my learner's permit yet," I said.

"So don't get in a wreck," Ma said.

I couldn't believe how cool Ma could be sometimes. I opened the door to let her in on the shotgun side like I was a gentleman, like I'd seen in the movies. She sat down and arranged her dress around her legs. I walked around the back of the car, shiny in the streetlight from our washing it, and got in the other side of the car and adjusted the seat, moving it back several notches so I could get my legs in comfortably and not be cramped under the steering wheel. I started the car and put it in gear, looked over my shoulder and pulled out onto the street, headed home.

An Evening When Nothing Happened

DINNER WAS FINISHED. MY MOTHER was done with the dishes. She went into the living room and turned on the radio; it was time for one of her regular programs, "The Longines Symphonette." I went outside and sat on the porch steps to hear the quiet and to watch evening come.

The air was hot and still, and after a while, I got up and dragged the hose to the driveway, turned the water on, and sprinkled the dust, my thumb held tight over the end of the hose. A clear fan of water spread before me like glass. The dust gave off a smell of age and decay, its color turned from near-white to brown, water drops left pock marks like craters on the moon.

I ran water on my arms and legs and bare feet. It cooled

me and the dampened dust cooled the air around the house and made the evening feel clean.

Crickets sang from across the driveway where the land was lower and the air cooler. I went back to the steps and sat looking across the field and I listened to the crickets' song. The fragrance of hot dry grass drifted on the evening breeze and heat waves shimmered up just above the ground. A rosy haze gathered over the field, fading to pink at the horizon; the sun was setting, proof that the Earth was turning.

Once in a while, I could hear my mother's radio program through the open windows, tender music that made me wonder what loneliness really is. I felt happy and I felt sad at the same time. I thought about love, wondered if I would fall in love someday like people in songs do. I felt like crying, but there was no reason to cry. No real reason. Nothing real I could think of to cry about.

It was just an evening when nothing happened at the Home Place except that I sat on the porch steps and watched the sun set, proof the Earth was turning, and waited for the evening to cool so I could go to bed.

A Dance in the Garden

 ALL THE SIGNS THAT SAID "END OF summer" were there—tired leaves dropping from trees, thistle seeds with parachutes gliding above the land, unseen spider threads in the air, sticky when they drifted against my face and arms. These were the signs that summer was over, but I didn't read them. Didn't want to read them, and the end of summer caught me by surprise.

What I thought was that building the garden at the Home Place with Gene would go on forever. That's what I wanted to believe, but that's not what happened. I found myself in a classroom hearing about theorems and axioms and plane geometry, reading about Kate in *The Taming of the Shrew*, still not getting to the sexy part even though the cover of the book showed a man spanking a woman he had turned over his knee. I wasn't talking to Gene much or swimming in the irrigation canal these days. It was gym and jock straps now.

I didn't read the signs that Gene was leaving, either. The tips on how to put the garden to bed for winter. The advice to mulch the bleeding heart, *Dicentra formosa*, to mark the peonies with little flags so as not to dig them up by accident in the spring. The directions on planting tulips and daffodils and China lilies late in the fall. How to plant dahlias next spring, and glads—it all went by me as lessons on how to be a gardener and none of it sounded to me like "I'll be leaving soon and you'll be on your own in the garden then." Which is how I should have heard it if I'd heard it right.

This is what I finally heard one afternoon when Gene and Ma and I were sitting under the arbor in the perennial garden drinking lemonade and looking over the pit, where a flock of valley quail grazed in the wildflowers Gene had seeded.

"I'm going to be leaving Stockton," Gene said.

Ma and I looked at him, looked at each other.

"Leaving Stockton?" Ma said.

I couldn't think what to say. I'd heard "leaving Stockton" clear enough, so I didn't need to ask to hear it again like Ma did.

"The University of California hired me to work at the botanic garden in Berkeley," he said. "I couldn't pass it up. It's a great opportunity. I'll really miss you two." He took a drink of lemonade.

I took a drink of lemonade from my glass, too.

"I don't know what to say, Gene," Ma said. "It does sound like a wonderful opportunity. I'm happy for you."

Ma stood up and got the pitcher of lemonade and refilled our glasses. She set the pitcher down and stood looking over the wildflowers in the sunken garden, not too grandiose.

"You're like one of the family around here. You helped me . . ."

Ma paused, unable to say more, knew what she wanted to say, probably even had the words, but her throat wouldn't let her say them.

"Helped me with much more than the garden," she said. "Helped us." She turned and looked at me.

I nodded. My face felt hot. Not all red, I hoped.

"Berkeley?" I said. "That's a ways away."

"Not so far," Gene said. "I'll come visit you every once in a while, Ace. Have to check up, make sure you're doing a good job here, not killing off plants, not getting too grandiose."

"You won't be back much if you're in Berkeley," I said.

"Yes I will," Gene said. "Every once in a while, and we'll get together, have some pizza. Maybe you and your ma can come visit me down there beside the bay and the big city. We can go looking at gardens, give those rich folks pointers on how to do it right."

Gene was making it sound all lighthearted and fun, but I was feeling like the kid in *Shane*. Felt like running down the road after the hero on the horse who saved the family from the cattle ranchers, waving my arms, calling, "Shane, Shane, come back, Shane," only it was Gene I called and it was all inside, not called aloud at all. No sound coming out. I took another drink of lemonade.

It was Saturday afternoon and Ma was in her bedroom pampering herself before going on a date with George. I was lying down in my room reading *The Taming of the Shrew*, didn't want to seem too stupid on Monday morning, Miss Nakamura walking up and down the aisle between desks, asking questions about Kate and Petruchio, Fair Bianca, too. Shakespeare: Greek to me.

What was on my mind, though, was Gene Tole, his leaving town, moving to Berkeley. Felt like a weight had dropped into my chest and caught there. Needed to cry. But why should I? A man my mother hired to build a garden, a stranger until he showed up to work. No way I could understand. No way.

The person who could help me understand was leaving, but maybe he could help me see what was wrong, why I felt so terrible. Gene, the only person to talk to.

Early that morning, Ma had said, "I'm going out to dinner with George tonight and perhaps to a late movie if there is time. Maybe you can get together with Dexter?"

"Parkie? You've got to be kidding."

I decided right then that I would visit Gene that evening. I would go to his house while Ma was out with George. It was okay, fine to say good-bye to Gene again, maybe my last chance to talk with him for a long while, last chance to see him.

I didn't want it to seem as though I was rushing Ma out the door that evening, but I couldn't wait for her to leave. When she finally got into George's car and they pulled out of the driveway, I jumped in the shower downstairs and scrubbed up good. Washed my hair with Ma's shampoo. Upstairs in my room, I picked out a pair of Levi's, dark blue, not faded yet, and a brand-new shirt, light blue with wide maroon stripes, long sleeves.

The more I thought about visiting Gene, the more excited I got. I wondered what Gene was doing right now— maybe he was getting dressed for the evening, too. I pulled my Jockey shorts on, tucked myself in, and jiggled to get a comfortable fit, everything in its own place. I watched myself dress in the mirror, pulled my maroon striped shirt on slowly over my shoulders, adjusted it around my body, a little dusting of hair across my chest, around my nipples, under my arms now. Buttoned the shirt up, looking in the mirror while I did it. I turned away to get my Levi's off the bed.

In my mind I saw myself riding up to Gene's house on my bike, Gene sitting on his front porch, getting up, saying how glad he was to see me, wouldn't I come in, talk with him while he packs his last few things. Following him into the house, through the door to his bedroom, standing in his room, holding back by the door, leaning against the frame, soft light, his clothes spread out ready to pack, personal things, too—razor, amber-colored cologne in heavy glass, comb, silver-handled brush, silk vest.

I looked in the mirror in my room and combed my hair a new way, parted it, the part not working worth a damn in my curly hair. Looked at myself dressed in my new shirt—not bad, I thought. Took a rag to my loafers, buffed them up.

Out in the barn, I tried not to bump into anything dusty, which was just about everything, while I pushed my old balloon-tire Schwinn to the driveway. I rode from the barn out the driveway, pedaled along the shoulder of the road, careful of loose gravel next to the pavement. I was soaring in the fresh evening air, my shirtsleeves fluttering against my arms, across my back, feeling good. Past the curve in the road by the Pasacco girls' place and a quarter mile more to the intersection of Highway 50. I turned right, followed the road alongside Mormon Slough, over the railroad tracks, past the train trestle over the slough, and on until I came to Golden Gate Avenue. There I turned the bike north, riding into a neighborhood, gust of wind every once in a while when a car passed. I went along tree-lined streets past East Main Street and a few blocks beyond to where houses were less frequent, with vacant lots between them, the area where Vivian Bowers lived just as I remembered it.

Then just ahead were huge oak trees, smaller lacy trees beneath them, flowering vines falling over a wood fence and Vivian's garden gate. Beyond the gate, behind Vivian's house, was Gene's small house. I knew it was there, tucked away in her garden.

The Schwinn was still rolling when I jumped off, guiding it to the corner of Vivian's garage. I pushed the bike behind some shrubs next to the garage. I brushed my pants and shirt with my hands, felt fresh. My breath came hard from the ride, and I stood beside the gate in the soft evening air.

When I was breathing regular again, like I could talk in a full sentence if I needed to, I opened the gate and went in. Along the path, placed every so often, were stubby candles in small glass jars. Candlelight caught in leaves, wavered there, fluttered away, made the garden alive; it seemed to dance.

All background was lost in darkness and shadow, dusk having passed into deep, dark, blue, and even that blocked by the trees overhead. I walked slowly toward the back of the garden along the path between shrub beds and trees, caught in the delight of the candles.

Just as I got to the hedge and the opening in it that led to Gene's house, I heard music, and once in a while laughter. For a moment, I stood by the hedge uncertain whether to go on. Gene was not alone. There were other voices, talking and laughing.

I went on, though, walked through the opening in the hedge, and there was Gene's house all lit up, windows warm with yellow light, and strung across the front porch of his house were Japanese lanterns, glowing with light from within. So pretty. A magic place, a joy to look at.

What I wanted to do then was just drop to the ground and crawl under some shrub. Disappointment hit me that hard. I couldn't think.

I needed to see Gene again, see him alone to tell him good-bye, to ask him for help. I needed him to help me understand why I felt the way I felt.

But there was a party going on, Gene's going-away party. I knew it, and who did I think I was, not invited, what kind of friend of his that I could just show up, crash his party?

There was another way to think about it, though. Perhaps I could be part of the party, join in, maybe Gene would be glad to see me and I could meet his other friends. Maybe he just forgot to invite me. I began to feel differently.

I decided to look, check it out.

The dark secrecy of the hedge was behind me and I moved close to the house. Stood under an apple tree, its branches heavy with apples and low to the ground. Through the side window in the house I saw three men sitting around a table drinking and talking. One of them wore a red T-shirt with suspenders to hold up his pants. Away from the table, a man with short dark hair leaned on the wall next to a door, the kitchen beyond. The man with short hair held a beer bottle in one hand and smoked a cigarette with the other.

Then I saw Gene. He stood at a desk facing the wall and was putting a long-play record album on a record player. He lowered the needle arm and big-band music came on. Two of the men at the table laughed. One of them slapped the man with suspenders on the back and they all laughed again at a private joke.

Gene moved away from the record player and walked past the short-haired man standing in the doorway. Gene let his hand trail across the man's middle in a kind of light, passing embrace. The man lifted his hand to his mouth and inhaled deeply on his cigarette. I watched closely. Nothing much happened. The men at the table talked quietly.

Gene came back through the door with a beer in his hand. He leaned on the doorjamb close to the short-haired man, who was still smoking. Gene drank from his beer, then said something to him. The man drew on his cigarette. Gene set his beer down on the table. Then he reached over and took the cigarette out of the man's hand and put it in an ashtray on the table. The man with the dark hair put his beer down next to his cigarette. Then Gene put his arm around the man's shoulders and they moved to the center of the room. The men at the table watched; the one with suspenders said something and they all three laughed.

Gene held the dark-haired man's hand and they circled a moment, then Gene pulled the man close to him and put his arm around the man's waist and they danced holding each other tight, their faces almost touching, their bodies pressed together.

Two men from the table got up and danced, too.

I dropped down to my knees, dizzy. I couldn't watch. Put my head down to help me breathe.

Finally, the music changed. I looked up.

Gene stood in the center of the room holding the man with the dark hair in his arms, and they moved slowly, hardly moving at all, bodies together, and Gene had his mouth on the other man's, kissing him.

No idea how long I watched, not too long, I don't think. I was doubled over on the ground, felt like someone had just kicked me in the stomach, knocked the wind out of me, couldn't breathe.

A screen door slammed.

Thought, If only I could get away from here, if only I'd never come.

The man with suspenders walked out onto the front porch, stood in the soft light of the Japanese lanterns. He leaned against the pillar and smoked.

I stayed perfectly quiet, my eye on the man until he went back inside. Still watching the house, I got up on my haunches, then stood slowly, using my hands for support. I stayed bent over and walked like that softly from under the apple tree. I checked the house, then turned and ran quietly to the hedge, through the opening, and then out past the garden, running full speed at that point, hitting branches, tripping over shrubs. I grabbed my bike and pedaled standing up, pumping as hard as I could to get away. No sign that anyone had followed me. Just had to be away. Needed to be alone.

At the corner of Golden Gate Avenue and Main Street I stopped and got a drink of water at Peterson's Service Station, rinsed my mouth and splashed my face from the fountain. Leaned my back against the metal siding and stared at the quiet streets. Moon rising, light reflected off the pavement and white-painted houses. I couldn't think of what to do or where to go. Finally what sounded best was to go home. Be there. I got back on my bike and rode slowly along Highway 50, cars and trucks passing once in a while with a gust of wind. And I thought as I rode.

I'd tell no one about what had happened in Vivian's garden, tell no one about what I'd seen, what I'd learned about Gene Tole. I'd keep everything I knew to myself. Maybe someday I could understand. Understand why Gene kissed a man. Now I couldn't.

I looked back over my shoulder for traffic so I could cross Highway 50, turned left on Mariposa Road, practically home now.

Why would he do it? Kiss that man. Dance with him. Did he love the man with short dark hair? Men don't love men, not that way, I knew that much. But then I thought, I loved Gene Tole, wanted to be with him, always, had to admit it, but that was different. I don't know how, just different, and I was crying now, could hardly see the damn road, everything was so blurry, like riding my damn bike underwater.

When I first got home I put my bike in the barn and then held my head under the faucet by the back porch and let water run all over my hair, my face, cool myself down. I held my head like that for a while, turning it slowly back and forth. Doing that picked me up a bit. I pulled my shirt out where it was still tucked into my pants and dried myself off with the tails. Took myself some deep breaths, looked at the stars, a few puffs of clouds in the sky.

Ma was standing by the back door when I was ready to go in.

"I just got in a minute ago myself," she said. "Come on in. Want something to eat?"

"No," I said. But she set out a glass of milk and some cookies anyway and I ate them. Don't ask me why.

With no care about what I'd decided earlier—to keep quiet, not say anything—I blurted out the whole story, walked around the kitchen, couldn't sit, and blurted out every damn thing I could think of. I talked like a runaway tape recorder.

I told about my bike ride over to Gene's to visit. Told about the party, the three men sitting around the table, the music, the beer. I told about Gene dancing with a man, holding the man, kissing him.

"Why would he do that? Why would he?" I was crying again and Ma held me. Neither one of us spoke.

"I don't know what to say," Ma said, her voice quiet, tired-sounding. "People's lives are sometimes difficult." She paused. "It's hard to know why people do what they do. I wish I could explain it better for you, but I can't." She was quiet, held me for a while. Finally, she said, "It's late. We better get to bed. We can talk in the morning."

Ma gave me a couple aspirin and told me to try and get some sleep, but I couldn't sleep.

Couldn't stop thinking about Gene, about what happened, about what I'd seen. I gave up on the idea of sleep. Got out of bed, opened the window, and crawled through to sit awhile on the porch roof. The sky was patchy with clouds, moonlight shining through now and then. I sat naked on folded pajama bottoms, back against the wall, and thought.

Thought about Gene, mostly. Thought about how I felt about him, about how much I loved him. Couldn't figure love out. Loved my brother, Brad. But sometimes I didn't. Tried to love my father, even though I didn't feel loved back. Dad loved me, though, I guess. Ma said he did, I knew he must, just couldn't say so, couldn't show it.

Thought about Gene Tole's friend Chris Rudd and the way those two hugged in Luther Burbank's garden, so glad to be together, glad to be friends. Friends, I guess. Called *mariposa* by Pete, the old Mexican man at Luther Burbank's garden.

Clouds rolling away from the moon now, and the garden shining bright, prettier than in daylight, valley oak and black walnut, *Quercus lobata* and *Juglans nigra*, holding the moon caught in twigs and branches. Pea-gravel paths reflecting light, shadow of the arbor in the perennial garden hiding the sitting area, the terrace. The pit beyond filled with wildflowers, not too grandiose. The garden serene in the moonlight, the garden Gene and I built. Together.

I'd find Gene in the morning, go see him, before he left

for Berkeley, and when he moved to Berkeley to work at the botanic garden, I'd get on the bus every once in a while and go to Berkeley, too. I'd visit Berkeley, the botanic garden and Gene Tole.

How could I love Gene Tole? I wondered. A man. How could I not love him? Couldn't figure love out. Too crazy. But I would, I knew, I would figure love out. I'd figure love out and I'd live by the kind of love that was right for me.